# GREENHORNS

# Also by the Author

## Fiction

*The Crater*

*The Return of Henry Starr*

*Abe: A Novel of the Young Lincoln*

## Non-Fiction

*Regeneration Through Violence:*
*The Mythology of the American Frontier, 1600-1860*

*The Fatal Environment:*
*The Myth of the Frontier in the Age of Industrialization,*
*1800-1890*

*Gunfighter Nation:*
*The Myth of the Frontier in Twentieth Century America*

*Lost Battalions:*
*The Great War and the Crisis of American Nationality*

*No Quarter: The Battle of the Petersburg Crater, 1864*

*Long Road to Antietam: How the Civil War Became a Revolution*

*So Dreadfull a Judgment:*
*Puritan Responses to King Philip's War, 1676-1677*
[with James K. Folsom]

# GREENHORNS

*Stories*

Richard Slotkin

*Leapfrog Press*
*Fredonia, New York*

Greenhorns © 2018 by Richard Slotkin

Published in 2018 in the United States by
Leapfrog Press LLC
PO Box 505
Fredonia, NY 14063
www.leapfrogpress.com

Printed in the United States of America

Distributed in the United States by
Consortium Book Sales and Distribution
St. Paul, Minnesota 55114
www.cbsd.com

Author photo courtesy of Bill Burkhardt


First Edition

Library of Congress Cataloging-in-Publication Data

Names: Slotkin, Richard, 1942- author.
Title: Greenhorns / Richard Slotkin.
Description: First edition. | Fredonia, NY : Leapfrog Press LLC, 2018.
Identifiers: LCCN 2018020621 (print) | LCCN 2018021541 (ebook) | ISBN 9780979641596 (e pub, kindle) | ISBN 9781935248996 (pbk.)
Classification: LCC PS3569.L695 (ebook) | LCC PS3569.L695 A6 2018 (print) | DDC 813/.54--dc23
LC record available at https://lccn.loc.gov/2018020621

For Iris, as ever—and also for Joel, Caroline and Jack.

# Contents

The Gambler                                               9

The Other Side                                           40

Honor                                                    49

Milkman                                                  80

Children, Drunks and the United States of America        94

Uncle Max and Cousin Yossi                              122

Greenhorn Nation: A History in Jokes                    161

Acknowledgements                                        177

Reader's Guide to Greenhorns                            179

Author                                                  183

# The Gambler

In Brooklyn before the war, the kosher butchers used to meet at the wholesaler's every Monday an hour before dawn. The hollow cavern of the loading dock boomed their greetings. The chilled air floated the bitter copper-penny reek of stale blood. Long rows of empty meat hooks swung from rails overhead. When the refrigerator trucks pulled in the wholesaler's men would heave and hang the stripped hollow beef carcasses on the meat hooks, the chain-belt would haul them swaying across the face of the platform where the butchers stood, checking for the kosher stamp and the Agriculture stamp, making their bids and tagging what they bought.

While they waited for the trucks the butchers would gather in the office. The faded blue eagle of the National Recovery Administration still spread its wings on the office wall, although it was a year since the neighboring Schechter Poultry Company and the Nine Old Men on the Supreme Court had wrung its neck like that of a sick chicken. But in the picture frame below it President Roosevelt's grin still held his cigarette holder at a jaunty angle.

Manny would take out a deck of cards and ripple it and they'd haul up chairs and sit down to a few hands of draw poker, nickel and dime: at the table the "regulars," Manny and Itzik and Berel and Koppy and Aaron, and the kibitzers standing behind their chairs. The dealer would throw down cards, and they'd take the hands they'd been dealt as a challenge or an insult—

"This he gives me? This from a friend?"

9

# Richard Slotkin

"The hole in the bagel, that's what I give you," says Manny throwing in a nickel and the betting goes around.

They draw cards: three each for Manny, Itzik and Berel, two for Koppy, bets a nickel, one card for Aaron who tops the nickel with a dime: "Grease the wheels and the wagon goes."

"The man plays for a straight, he should be so lucky," says Manny throwing in his hand, Itzik drops with "*I* should be so lucky," and Berel too, "Your *enemies* should be so lucky."

Koppy and Aaron: bet, raise, call . . . show cards. Aaron has missed the straight.

Berel says, "Aaron—with all due respect, who throws money at a straight *inside?*"

And he answers: "*Az me leygt arayn, nemt min aroys.*" What you put in, you take out.

The truth is, if three times a year he takes out more than he puts in it's a lot. But he can't leave it alone. Look at him there, a little man with a head like a cannonball, tight-curled steel gray hair cropped close, the big nose drooping over the grizzled moustache— he laughs with his mouth, gives a dig takes a dig, it would be a shame to let a friendly game become serious. But he sits hunched to the table and his little black eyes are not laughing. They search the cards for the luck he lost somewhere between the Other Side and Brooklyn, and what happened to it? Twenty-five years in the *goldene medineh* and he's still as thin as a starved chicken. Where was the "corporation"—the paunch of a successful man—he had a right to expect? Where was his *lebn*, the life that ought to have been his?

Later, with the sun well up, when he comes back to the shop having put a big dent in the profits he hasn't yet made from the meat he went to buy, Sarah will throw an eye at him. "Home from the fair with dust in his pockets."

"What I went to get, I got." A man is not accountable to a woman.

She doesn't blink. There are things in this world to be frightened

# Greenhorns

of, but he is not one of them. So she answers: "*A nekhtiger tug.*"
Yesterday's day—that's what you went to find. Not even God can
give you back yesterday's day.

As a young man on the Other Side he was lucky, and he knew it.

When he was an infant both of his parents died of cholera in
a muddy *shtetl* east of Mogilev. He brought nothing to the Jewish
people but hunger and cries, which were not in short supply in that
province. His mother's cousin's family took him in for a season,
then passed him on to some other relation, and so on.

You say to yourself, what kind of luck is that? Because you're
American. You open your eyes in the morning and expect to live a
life, to earn your bread and savor its taste, to know your grandparents, to see your parents grow old before you, to see your children
and grandchildren grow to maturity, each in their proper season.
But on the Other Side it's not a question whether sickness and
death will visit you—it's what happens after you survive the visit
that marks you lucky or unlucky.

When Aaron was six a butcher from the next town, a widower
with no male children, took him in as apprentice and foster son.
They got along. The old man was not much for conversation, but
the boy had a mouth, a clever laughing mouth under a big fleshy
nose that hung down like the nose of a horse. He was short as a
stump and had to stand on a block to use the cleaver, but he had
small strong deft hands and a sharp eye. Over the years he learned
how to gut a chicken cleanly with delicate flicks of the knife, never nicking the bead-small glands whose gall could spoil the meat;
to split chops and clods off a beef with his cleaver, and then slice
and trim you out a steak, or a lean brisket for boiled beef. He even
learned the knack of removing the sinew and veins to render loin
meat kosher. His foster father died when he was fourteen, leaving
him only that skill and the tools with which to exercise it: the silky
whetstone, the pair of cleavers heavy and light, the bone-saw, the
knives for boning and trimming and slicing—already worn thin by

11

years of honing, instruments to be cossetted in a wrap of cloth-soft leather, never to touch bread or paper, never to draw unclean blood.

Three years later he was working in another man's shop in another little muddy Jewish town only a mile or two closer to Mogilev, when Sarah came in to pick up an order. As soon as they set eyes on each other they laughed—as look-alike as if they were brother and sister, which thank God they were not: eye-to-eye for height, the same round head with wiry curls, the same lumpy nose, the same snap in the black eyes, the same wry lift of one eyebrow, the same laugh-lines around the mouth and eyes. She was an orphan herself, taken in as a servant by a distant relation, a grain-dealer with money to spend on a household. Even as a servant in that house she lived better than most people: look at the cleanliness of the hand-me-down dress, the shoes with new soles cobbled to the cracked uppers. What could he offer but an equal share in his poverty and the place beside him in his broken-backed bed in the loft over the shop? That and the fact that whenever he set his eyes on her he was so happy he had to laugh, and she had to laugh too. A pair of fools with no sense.

So he threw his poverty on the table against the comfort of that house in which she was a servant. "The Lord led us out of the House of Bondage," he'd say. "You can't eat your fill at another woman's table." She'd match him word for word. A woman, she'd say, could fall in love as easily with a rich man as with a poor one. And he'd laugh: "In the bath house you can't tell poor from rich." What a romantic! But how can you say in words what is in a laugh?

His eyes burnt like coals, warm—sometimes a biting heat. Her black eyes had sparks in them, and yet in their shape a sad droop at the corners. And with those eyes she would look straight into his, and look and look.

"What do you see in there?" he asked her.

She lifted one eyebrow: "I see my children," she said.

His heart jumped and began pounding to get out of his chest.

# Greenhorns

"In your eyes I see my children," she said slowly, "and I see my grandchildren."

When the grain merchant withheld his approval, they eloped to the next small muddy Jewish town on the road to Mogilev. A wager: on one side the good will of her "family" and of his employer, the reputation he'd earned and the trade he'd won in that community; on the other laughter and an eye full of children. *Spiel korten.* Play the cards.

They lived from hand to mouth at first, but the hand had its cunning and the mouth was clever—a joke for the man, a deft compliment for the woman, so the customers took pleasure in doing business with him. Starting with nothing, with less than nothing, taking what was dished out and making the best of it, learning a lesson or two on the way, no great wisdom no great folly, working for this one and that they managed to squeeze a small capital out of their living.

A customer told them about a tiny *shtetl* named Khashchavata, lost out in the vast countryside northeast of Mogilev, where the butcher wanted to sell out and go to America. The town enjoyed a degree of poverty somewhat above average for the district. Its remoteness from the cities preserved it from the attention of the authorities, the murderous rage of the pogroms and the "protection" of the police. Even the *khapers*, who were paid a bounty by the government for every Jew they could grab for the military—and were punished if they failed to deliver their quota—thought the town too small and out of the way to bother with.

Aaron jumped at the chance, with just enough cash to buy the little shop and good enough credit to stock it with meat from week to week.

Twelve years go by and look: from nothing he and Sarah have a *lebn*—a living, a life, how do you say it? A shop on the square, a house with three rooms, the smell of cooked cabbage, meat stewed with carrots and beans and garlic, crackling bits of fatty chicken skin browned crisp with browned onions. When he breathed, when he ate his meals he had a woman by him, a companion in whose eyes he had charm and even beauty. A woman who bore him three sons—three circumcisions, three to labor beside him in his strength and sustain him in his old age and say Kaddish when he passed, that his blood should not just vanish into the earth, that his name should be heard and not forgotten in this place: "Aharon ben Yoisef Rubinow." Even the government now considered him a "Useful Jew," a man of skill and property and not some *lumpen* beggar or shit-shoveler.

A hardworking man—but also a lucky man: how many work like horses and eat like mice?

In his heart he was satisfied, but he would not give that feeling words, not even with Sarah, who thought him a man stingy with praise. It's not a good idea to presume on God's favor—He might decide to teach you a lesson in humility. On the other hand, it doesn't do to seem ungrateful—because if you whine about the luck God sends you He's liable to send you worse. So if you asked Aaron how he was doing he would say, "It could be worse, with God's blessing."

So look at him now: a solid little man with a head like a cannonball and a nose to smell the world with, stepping out of his own door of an evening to sniff the air and feel entitled to it. A man among his fellows: for from his doorway he can see other men like himself standing at their doors, "A good evening to you," solid citizens of their little street.

One evening in the week these men would sit down at a table together and play some cards, not big money, a kopeck or two. It was a ritual, like taking a bite of honeycake and a glass of wine after prayer on the Sabbath, a small symbolic luxury, an affirmation that they were not paupers, with God's help they could spend a little for their pleasure. They played some *preferenz* and twenty-one, and Yankel the tailor—who had spent seven years making his bundle in America—taught them American draw poker.

# Greenhorns

This was a game that Aaron loved, it engaged him, it woke him up. It was a game that showed an understanding of life. With twenty-one, chance was everything—as if to say that nothing a man does will make a difference, that neither Creator nor Judge exists and the world is just a senseless tumbling. With *preferenz* everything depended on the skill of the player, a good head could turn a handful of chickenshit into a glass of tea—yet how often in this world do the wise and good actually receive according to their gifts?

But in poker the mix of skill and luck was a perfect reflection of life as Aaron understood it. Success in poker demanded a difficult balancing: one must *rely* on luck, and yet not *count* on it—*vershtays*? In the same way that one trusts in God, but bears always in mind that you cannot simply depend upon His good will. There was a narrow line to be walked between boldness and presumption. God threw all sorts of crap in your way, but every now and then for a joke He'd drop in a chance of good luck. It was as bad, as offensive to refuse such a gift—to fail (through cowardice or false modesty) to seize and use it for all it was worth—as it was to tempt God by presuming on His favor through reckless or spendthrift play.

From poker it came to him that luck was a form of grace. You couldn't make it come, or pray it on yourself, but if you played with skill and care and discipline and modesty you might put yourself where luck could find you out. And then if you had an eye to see, a nose to smell, and the *kishkes* to make your play . . . *ha*!

Aaron thought well of the Americans for inventing such a game. But he was skeptical about America: a Promised Land, a *goldene medineh*—these struck him as the sort of promises traveling salesmen and gypsies make. Yankel the Tailor reinforced that skepticism. As a young man he had followed the promise to the Streets of Gold and, as he said, found they were actually paved with rocks and horse-shit. He had lived there seven years, made a little capital by slaving over a sewing-machine and starving himself, and came back to live and raise his children—and lately his

15

grandchildren—in a Jewish world. Others stayed in America, professing assurance they would make their fortunes. For Yankel, this was the pretense of men unwilling to admit a colossal mistake. "They don't want tailors there, just a foot to work the pedal and a hand to push the cloth. You don't make a suit of clothes or a dress, but shirtwaist shirtwaist shirtwaist, the way one tasks an apprentice learning the trade. You live one on top of another like piled-up potatoes, with your neighbor's ass hanging over your soup-bowl. Not even the air in your lungs is your own—the Italian by the window breathes a breath and passes it down the row to the rest of you grinding away at the machines."

Lots of men threw everything into a bindle and hit the road for America, betting their lives and their families on the chance of a big success in New York. What risk for what return? It seemed to Aaron that his luck was good right here, he would be a fool to press it, to ask more of the cards than cards could give. Here he had his house and shop, the wife of his heart, a respected place in the community, able to honor his parents by standing in the synagogue to say Kaddish for them, with three sons to do the same for him—

—Yoisef, the eight-year-old—named for Aaron's father—with his mother's curly hair and her impish smile. Already he would sit on the floor of the shop, making little mountains among the sawdust on the floor, waiting to jump up and seize his chance to turn the crank of the cast iron mill that ground beef-ends for sausage. Already he was eager to get his hands on the tools he would one day inherit, along with the shop and the trade his father had gathered for him.

—Chaim, two years younger, named for Sarah's father—he'd learn the trade and make his way with skill and diligence, and who knew? With a little luck maybe marry a girl with a bit of a dowry, that he too should start his life with a little property.

—And little Binyamin, newly born and named to honor the butcher who had taken Aaron in and taught him the trade by which he lived and prospered. With a father and two brothers earning the money perhaps he would be sent to school to become a horse-doctor or book-keeper for a rich merchant.

All this Aaron had, and his years as well. *Farlorene yor'n iz erger vi verlorene gelt*—lost years are worse than lost money, and if he was not rich in rubles he was still rich in years, in the prime of his life, his short beard soft and curling, Sarah still with skin soft as an apricot. Slowly, slowly, he and Sarah would grow old with honor here among people who knew them, "A *gut yontiff* to you Reb Aharon. . . ."

Why spend years in wandering when all he could want was already his?

In September of 1902 his luck was in. Just after Yom Kippur a relative of his foster father wrote to tell him of a very nice butcher shop in the city of Mogilev, whose owner was putting all his equipment and fittings up for a quick sale. Aaron arranged to ride the twenty miles with Isaac Drob the drayman, who was carrying a load of grain bags to the city. Ten miles out of town the horse threw a shoe, and till Drob shaped a new one and hammered it on the day failed them, and they had to spend the night in the woods sleeping under the wagon.

Next morning early they pulled out into the road, and here came a man, a Jew by the look of him, stumbling toward them waving his arms in circles like a madman, "Turn around, turn around, get going . . . but wait for me! don't leave me!" Isaac Drob hauled the horses' heads around. If a Jew in that country was running away from something he probably had good reason. But Aaron reached down to give the man a hand up on the rolling wagon.

"A pogrom?"

The man shook his head. "No, but bad enough. There's a conscription in Mogilev. All Jewish men between the ages of so-and-so to report immediately, and in case you're hard of hearing the *khapers* kick the door down and drag you out into the street. Single, married, only sons, 'Useful Jews' . . . the whole kettle of fish."

"You'll stay by us," the drayman told him, "nobody bothers us out in the sticks."

"Maybe not," the man replied, "but if I can raise the cash I'm buying a ticket to America."

And just like that, for Aaron the world turned itself inside out. It was true that neither pogroms nor *khapers* had found the path to Khashchavata—yet. But luck does not last forever. To think otherwise is not only foolish, but disrespectful to God. A man must know when he has been given his full measure, and then be man enough to leave the table to others. The signs were dark, the meanings twisted: if not for the "bad" luck with the horseshoe, the "good" luck of the sale in Mogilev would have given him over to the *khapers*. And for a Jew the difference between conscription and a Cossack raid was the difference between slow death and fast. The term of service was fifteen years, and who ever met a Jew that lasted that long? He saw as in a vision the gutted carcasses of beef stripped to waxy white fat and red stinking flesh, and it was himself he saw, no swift sharp *shokhet*'s blade to cut his throat mercifully clean and quick, but skinned alive and gutted and swung on a hook. And for what, for who? A Tsar in Saint Petersburg who dipped his snuff with a gold spoon and ate caviar while his people killed and ate each other—or more precisely, killed the Jews and devoured their substance.

His luck let him escape this time—but what of the next?

He tried to imagine himself a concealment. Under the bed then, or in a closet, or the outhouse, live like a turtle, keep your head in the shell, breathe nothing but your own stink. He would become a negligible quantity, a ghost, without hunger or need, invisible. Who would bother to look for someone so unimportant he could scarcely be said to exist?

But even if he succeeded hiding out, evasion was a crime, the authorities would seize his store and house and everything he owned. With no property, the law would not permit his family to live in this town or district, his wife and sons would be cast out to starve their way from poorhouse to poorhouse.

# Greenhorns

Besides, he's not a ghost, he's a man. And a man they can find, those bastards. They'll haul him out from under the bed or out of the closet or the outhouse, and they'll kick his Jewish ass and shame him before his wife and sons in his own house and haul him off to die in the snow, killing human beings for Tsar Nikolai, may his bones be ulcerated, may his marrow rot.

No: to have missed conscription by the width of a horseshoe was as much luck as any Jew could have in Russia.

And so he must run, get away where the Tsar can't lay a hand on him.

Run where? To *America*. Where else does a man run?

But America? You might as well go take a jump off the world. He knew as little of America as he knew of Death—maybe less. He didn't want America. What he wanted was *this* life, everything just as it was right now—not any single part but all of it, to see, to smell, he will hold this life in his two hands with a grip like an iron vise!

But if he holds tight he holds nothing: the Tsar's men will pry him loose and carry him off to die. If he would have his life he must take the chance of losing it.

So he went to talk to Yankel, to sound him out. What was wrong with America that he didn't stay once he got there?

A shrug. "I didn't leave because I can't stand hard work. It's true they sweat you sick to earn a dollar, but what you earn you can spend as you like. You live in a house where the rooms are stacked one on the other, like chickens in a chicken coop—but you live, without pogroms or conscription."

So then was it the *goyim*—they were worse than here?

Now Yankel smelled something: *Oho! A young man with an idea in his head*! But he answered as if they were just passing the time. "Yid'n they're not. But as goyim, they're all right. A Russian or a Pole will cross the street to insult a Jew, and beggar himself to do you harm. A German wipes you off like dogshit from his shoe.

A Frenchman or a British looks through you like you're not there—unless you get between him and the wind. But the Americans? They look at a Jew and they point and laugh and call you 'Ikey' or 'Izzy' and then they go about their business. And the laugh? It's the same laugh they give a Polack or an Irish or a Chinaman. Only a Negro they treat the way a Russian treats a Jew."

"Well, I'm not a Negro!"

"Not yet you're not!" And looked Aaron in the eye: "You're thinking of lighting out, aren't you?"

"What should I wait for? To grow like an onion with my head in the dirt? To raise children for the *khapers* to grab?"

Yankel shrugged. "Who can say anything to that?" Then he became serious: "You're not a fool, so let me tell you the truth exactly. That the streets are not paved with gold you know. But a living can be made there, by you as well as the next man. It's what you get *from* the living. . . ."

Aaron threw up his hands. Why was Yankel turning his head around? "From a living you get a living, what else is there to say? I know how to work. I'll make my way."

Yankel screwed up his face with the effort of explanation: "Seven years I lived there. My brother is there ten, and he lives there yet. Five years he worked till he could bring his wife and children over. Do you know how far away is Russia from America? Not just miles—days, weeks, months. How many years till you bring them over—two, three, five . . . ten? And what are you to them for all those years? A hole in the air where you used to be. And what are they to you? You'll meet again as strangers."

Aaron rolled his eyes. "They're my wife and my children, they'll know me."

What can one man tell another? But Yankel pushed a little harder. "Let it happen as you say. You may be as lucky as the next man, or luckier. But even so: shall I tell you what will be your portion? You'll be a stranger there all your life, you'll live and die without a place. You'll shovel shit, and shlep burdens like an ox, and wither like a tree without roots so your children should live a life—but you won't live it. You'll hammer yourself into the floor like a board, and your children will step on your head as they walk out the door."

Aaron understood: this was the truth of it—as Yankel knew it. And it came to him with force that if he went he must leave Sarah and his Kaddish and his babies where the Tsar, may worms crawl in his brain, could lay his hands on them. . . .

But if America was anything like what they *say* of America! Sure, it went bad for Yankel and his brother. But for another it might be different. *You can't take out if you don't put in.* As long as there are Jews a man won't starve. And if he doesn't starve he can make for his wife and children a place *in* America, and bring them over, and have them again, have all of *this* again, just as it was now. Only *safe*. Not air and smoke for the Tsar to blow away, but a *lebn* rooted in the ground like trees. And all his years, and all her years, and all their children's years still stretching on before them full of health and pleasure. What was a little time lost out of all that life to come? A few coins thrown in the pot, and then you can play your cards. If he stayed here his life was lost—what more than that could he lose on the road to America? And if he got there . . . *You'll hammer yourself into the floor, like a board for your children to step on?* He gave Yankel a grin: "What else should a man do with his life?"

Yankel gave him up with a smile and a shake of the head. "Of course you'll go, and God be with you. I'll write on a paper the address of my brother in New York. . . ."

When he came home that evening Sarah took one look and turned away from him. If she looked she would have to see, and she didn't want to see, that in his mind he had already chosen some terrible thing.

"I'm going," he said. "I'll send money when I can."

"Going where? "

"Away from here. America. . . ."

"America? You'll be my husband from America?"

"If I stay here they take me, and what becomes of you then?"

*"Men ken makhn dem kholem greyser vi di nakht."* A man thinks his dream is bigger than the night.

"I'm not dreaming. My eyes are open. A Jew here has one God and a million enemies. And we won't be separated. I'll find a place and send for you."

She knew it all as well as he, she accepted it, but into whose ears should she pour the bitterness of her heart if not his? "A wise head! If he stays he's gone, if he goes he don't leave us. With one ass he sits in *shul* and goes to the fair."

He nodded and said nothing. So the taste was bitter to her. What else should it be? But she would swallow it.

Then she asked, "When will I hear from you?"

"When you hear from me you'll hear."

"I'll be a grass widow. You'll disappear and I'll be alone till my days fail me."

"Sha," he said softly. "You'll be my wife in America. We'll live together till we can't tell night from morning. We'll go into the ground together."


Arrangements were quickly made. Sarah would sell the shop and its gear, the blocks and the counter and the hooks—the other butchers in the district would see she got something for it. The house he "sold" to Yankel for ten rubles—so the authorities could not seize it if he failed to answer a summons for conscription. He had spoken to Chaim Grozner, who had the other shop in town—Sarah could pluck and singe chickens for him, he'd see she had money to live on. How long could the journey take—six months, a year?

He left before sun-up. He kissed his wife, and bent to Yoisef, the little man of eight, the Kaddish with curly hair and his mother's eyes. "I'm going away, you understand? To find us a better town than this. You understand? I don't know how many days till you can come there too. While I'm gone, you are the man of the house."

The little man was not much concerned. How many days could there be? Papa goes away, and he comes back.

Wrapped in the blanket roll slung across his back and chest was all he had for the six thousand mile journey to America: one change of clothes, his knives and whetstone swaddled in soft leather, a piece of soap, in a cloth bag the thongs and frontlets with which on the Sabbath he would bind himself arm and brain to God. Sarah had sewed him a sash with one pocket for his *dokumentii* and another to keep his money in (less than half their savings to go with him, the rest to keep her till he could send) and wrapped it around his waist under the *tsitsis*, the white cloth with knotted fringes a good Jew wore next to his skin, to signify the shroud in which he would be wrapped on his last day above ground.

As Aaron went out the door he turned to look back. In the yellow light of candles he saw Sarah with the baby in the crook of her arm, and the little man Yoisef holding her other hand, and the small boy Chaim half-hidden behind her hip, and he fixed that image in his head and kept it there, like a Russky icon, a picture frozen in amber.

There were trains a man could take from Mogilev to the German border. But what he gained in speed he would lose in wherewithal, the money to buy passage to America. And on trains there were policemen who might look at one's papers and decide that Aharon ben Yoisef Rubinow, Useful Jew, butcher, of Mogilev Guberniya, had no business travelling at will across the Tsar's dominions, and should be fed to the press-gang. He must avoid the main roads, follow dark forest paths, the trees closing behind him like a wall of shadows.

Each step away from his home was like the draining of an ounce of blood. Better if he was an orphan again, leaving nothing behind, nothing to lose but his years. That thought blinded him like a blow between the eyes. He began to hurry, to rush toward the end, chased by a ghost of himself that must not catch him, pushing blindly through brush. Sprawled headlong, tripped up by a serpent of root.

He lay there with his belly in the dirt. What was the good of running? America was not the next *shtetl* on the road to Minsk. He had to mind his steps until he could see his way to America. Memory was a drag against his feet. To keep going he had to shut the door behind him tonight, and shut it again the next night, and again the night after.

So he put by the thought of everything that was dear to him. Here and now he is just *himself*: a hard little Jew with a bindle on his back, making his way by shifts and dodges, through the woods by day, circling wide around any town where there might be a policeman. He slips into Jewish *shtetls* away from the main roads and spends the night in the *hekdish*, the village poorhouse where the paupers and village idiots snore on benches. He meets in passing men like himself, *fussgeyers* walking west to America with their futures stowed in bindles slung across their backs.

He keeps walking, one foot in front of the other, as if painstakingly measuring in paces the distance to America. Each day has the intense spurious reality of a dream, absorbing Aaron completely in crucial details while somehow in the back of his head his true life is in suspense.

He is careful every day for the safety of his body, fully alert to the dangers that menace it, threaten to arrest its movement west. Yet he also feels insubstantial, a man of air floating, rushing like a cloud, detached from earth, from real things. The days no longer add up the way they did at home, Monday moving toward Sabbath, spring to summer, the richness of days accumulating in Sarah's body, their sons filling and rising toward their inheritance. Now on the journey each day stands alone—and yet, at the same time, rushes past with dizzying speed, and the memory of home is like the sight of a house seen from a train at night, the people in a lighted window frozen in the act of eating or was it praying? He knows that between himself and Sarah, and Yoisef and Chaim and Binyamin, distance is accumulating, time of absence piling up. But their image is an amber icon fixed in his head, petrified, unchanging, as if their lives must be suspended too, until he gets where he is going.

In this way he walked across White Russia and Poland in the dead of winter.

In March 1903, already five months out, he reached the German border. *If you can't go through, go around.* He paid a peasant smuggler to lead him at night through Polish potato fields and wade him through a swamp to another potato field which the peasant said was Germany. For all he could tell it was Poland, but the peasant already had his money. He started walking again, and it turned out to be Germany. So it was an honest peasant—another piece of luck.

Which allowed him to hike across Germany as he had already hiked across Poland and White Russia.

To Bremen: a wilderness of stone buildings and cobbled streets that stank of fish and brine and coal smoke and horse shit.

At the Jewish Agency in Bremen were Jews disguised as German burghers, with beards trimmed or clean-shaved, in tailored jackets and impeccable linen. The Agency gave the emigrants lodging in a sort of barrack they maintained. It would fix their documents, have a doctor look them over; in the meantime help them write letters to relatives waiting for them on the Other Side, and to those they left Back Home. And finally, see to it they weren't cheated when they bought their tickets.

How much for the tickets?

The Agency man named a figure in German marks, then translated it into an astronomical sum in rubles. But hot coals to Aaron was butter on the Agency man's tongue. Herr Rubinow was a butcher? They would find him a job till he could earn enough for his passage.

Aaron smiled a bitter smile. The deal had a smell to it. Back home it would take months to have that much cash simply pass across the counter into his hands, a year for any part of it to survive his expenses and find a home in his pocket. Considering what he needed to keep from starving in the meantime, to save up enough for his family's fare would take . . . an unimaginable time. This Jew with the look of a goy and the mind of a gypsy, he'd put Aaron to work like Laban put Jacob, and after seven years marry him to the *ugly* sister.

Of course he could always pawn or sell his knives. But to do that was to surrender the life he was risking everything to attain: to have again in America the shop and the trade and the life he enjoyed at home.

So in a city that smelt like a fish market he went to work for a German kosher butcher, a gigantic man who looked as if he could eat the contents of his shop at a sitting. At the end of the week Aaron, expecting *bubkes*—a handful of goat turds—received instead a small stack of bills and a clinking bunch of coins. Suddenly the sun came up in Bremen Germany and illuminated the world. Germany was not Russia any more than fat was lean. Here numbers multiplied like rabbits, in a week you earned a month's pay. The next day he went back to the Agency and wrote and had them post for him a letter to Sarah in which he enclosed a pay order (which the Agent explained to him when he tried to tuck a big banknote and some coins in the envelope).

Before him unfolded a vision of the generosity of God's world. And he himself had no mean part in it: sending back money to support his wife and children, the father and provider whose reach went out across a thousand miles.

He was still there in Bremen when, miraculous, a letter came back from her, addressed to him care of the Agency, written for her by Itzik Schreiber. She was fine. The boys were fine. There was talk of a war but nobody believed it but she was glad he was away where the army couldn't get him. It was a war against Chinamen from Japan. But nobody believed it.

# Greenhorns

Hen-scratches on a yellow page. Was it truly her voice? God in heaven how suddenly and hard he missed her! What with Germans and Agents and butchers and being so happy to send her money it had never occurred to him that, with what he'd earn working another six months at these wages, he could just send for her!

Well why not? America had rushed him off his feet. Now that he had them both on the ground again he had to ask himself why he shouldn't just stay where he was. He thought about the Jews at the Agency, well fed men in clean clothes, to him they were as good as any Germans. Yet they started out Jews. This was a possibility that Aaron had never imagined, but he did now. He would unwrap his knives, reveal his skill to the Germans, earn a good living, save his money, buy a German shop and earn a German living. It wasn't too soon to get Sarah and the boys out of Russia. Why risk the good he could see for an America he had never seen? What sort of play was it to lay down hard cash against a stranger's IOU?

Except. . . .

Except that others before him had seen Germany and kept going. Bremen smelt bad. And then: every Sabbath the cavalry came trotting up the street, clash clash clash, the troopers in black uniforms trimmed with silver looking straight ahead at nothing, like corpses on horseback. He knew Cossacks when he saw them—the German ones dressed and smelt better than the Russian kind, but they had that look, the dead man look that in a flash becomes the bloodthirsty glare and the gnashing of bared teeth.

So again the choice: leave the table with his winnings, or play another hand? Here was Germany, fat and generous before his eyes; and out there somewhere America, which could be anything at all but at least it was not *This*: the stink of fish and coal, the clash clash of dead-eyed horsemen in the streets.

If you're hanging by one foot, you might as well hang by both.

Instead of sending for her to come to him in Germany he counted his money, thanked his employer, and went down to the Agency to buy his steerage ticket on the S.S. *Bremen* bound for

# Richard Slotkin

New York. November, 1903—it had taken a full year just to get to the ocean.

Steerage: a fixation, an imprisonment in the daily details of eating (is it kosher is it *tref*, thin soup, meat like ragpickers' leavings, bread like compounded dust), communal shitting, the morning and evening prayers muttered in an atmosphere of stench and groaning, starving for a breath of air, trying to keep from vomiting when the floor heaves and drops away, a stink so thick and pervasive that it sinks into his skin, feverish dreams of falling, falling—the sense of being suspended in his days, moving neither forward nor back, and at the same time this terrible sense of rushing into the unknown. The golden picture of Sarah and Yoisef and Chaim and Binyamin is far behind him, but also ahead, a window towards which he is creeping through the dark.

A day dawns, gray and chilly and wet, and there across the steel-colored water is the colossal image of a woman carved out of metal, a torch in her hand and flames shooting out of her head. On the opposite side of the ship tall buildings climb like cliffs. New York. America.

A walk down a swaying ramp into a building smelling of carbolic and urine and sweat. Men behind tables, nurses behind the men. Questions. A man looks in your eyes. Then he looks in your ears. Then you open your mouth and he looks in that too, like a man buying a horse. Should he neigh? No, keep silent, the less you say the less you have to take back. In the end Aharon ben Yoisef Rubinow trades them his three names for two of theirs and walks out into the air and onto the ferry as Aaron Rubin.

He spends the first night with Yankel's New York brother, and between the brother and the Khashchavata Society *landsmanshaft* finds work and a tenement apartment. Actually it is just a piece of apartment, a bunk in a small room he shares with seven other men. You walk up six flights of stairs and down an airless yellow corridor,

# Greenhorns

open the door and in the first room is the Moskowitz family, husband and wife, two children and grandma; walk through to another door, good evening to the Rabinowitz brothers and their three cousins from Podolia, then the room for Aaron and the lucky seven, and beyond them yet another room—Jakobofsky family, eight in all, they have the longest walk but also the advantage of a window in the back wall, which Aaron's room lacks, so that when he wakes up in the middle of the night and hears the others sucking in deep and blowing it out he wonders whether they'll drain the air and drown him like fish, and he remembers Yankel's joke about the Italians breathing at the window and passing the air down the line of sewing-machine operators, ha ha, very funny.

At least he works in the open air, heaving and hauling beef carcasses on a loading dock at the Hudson River terminal, where the freight cars come in on the ferry from Jersey. From a kosher butcher, a man of skill, a businessman with his own shop, he's become a shlepper, work that could be done by any blockhead *boolvan* from the country. *If you can't do what you want, do what you can.* The knives stayed swaddled in their soft leather wrappings, and he kept them sharp for the day he could use them once again. If worse came to worst he'd sell or pawn them, but not until he had no more cards to play. In the meantime he smokes but one cigarette a day, and eats just enough to keep going—cabbage and onions he buys the day the grocer is ready to throw them out, a little meat and fat from the trimmings the butchers leave, fried in a pan on the stove that serves all four rooms. Not enough to get fat on, and nothing for the pleasure of its taste. He even sends a little money back to Sarah, though to do so delays the day when he can send enough to cover passage and travel expenses for her and the boys. But the thread that binds them stretches so long now, so long and thin, that he must make a little tug on it to convince himself she's still there, just as he left her, drenched in amber with one son in her arms and one by each hip.

He goes to the little upstairs loft of the Khaschavata *landsman-shaft* on Sunday, the goyisher Sabbath, in case a letter has come,

# Richard Slotkin

and if not at least he'll talk to his *landsleit*, to people who speak his kind of Yiddish, whose eyes remember the sights he has seen, and maybe he'll hear news of the old town. On a Sunday in winter 1904, as he's climbing the stairs a man comes charging up behind him and bangs him into the wall—he grabs a handful of coat, he'll give this oaf a going-over, but the man shows him a face transfigured with terror: "It's war!" he cries, "The Japs have sunk the Russian navy and they're ripping into each other like wolves!"

The man tears away and bounds up the stairs two at a time with Aaron hanging to the tail of his coat, and they burst in that room like a bomb. Yelling, cries, blabber, guessing, wishing, but through it all the same words, "I've heard nothing! nothing!" A waste of breath, no one knew anything. He stumbles downstairs again and out into the street.

Behind him the sound of their voices shrank to a rustling. A coal wagon drawn by two horses *clop clop* passed him at a brisk pace. Above the ranked windows of the houses rising tier after tier, in the slot above the street the American clouds drifted easily across the blue sky.

For weeks then he was like a man lost in fogs and mists, blundering into walls and bulks that seemed to materialize from nothing: the Russians winning, the Russians losing, Cossacks and peasants raging through the Pale of Settlement.

Aaron used whatever connections the *landsmanshaft* or its members had to try to contact Sarah, or at least get news of what was happening in the town. Nothing but scraps—then at last after weeks a letter, but written in a different hand: she's safe thanks to God, and the boys—too young for the *khapers*! But the conscription got Itzik Schreiber and also Chaim Grozner, so now she's running Grozner's store and cutting the meat, what meat the army leaves, and Yoisef with her, he cleans the chickens you should see his little hands make the feathers fly, they leave us alone but it won't last, get us out of here—either come back or get us out.

30

# Greenhorns

He sees in a flash of vision the terrible disorder of her life.

But what can he do except what he's already doing? With the war it's harder to get letters and money orders in and out, harder to get the papers you need to go from here to there let alone get living human beings across a border. You need agents, who know what to do and have pockets full of American cash to do it with, and the Khashchavata is a poor society, no big shots with capital to draw on, just a bunch of tailors and shoemakers and bakers and shleppers. He grabs every one of them by the lapels, but they all have their troubles, their own hostages and no money to pay the ransom.

No money, but his countrymen are rich in *rakhmones*, in compassion. One of them has an uncle in Brooklyn, a kosher butcher in Williamsburg, and the man speaks with the uncle on Aaron's behalf. Liebowitz is twenty years in the country, he's built up a good business but his older son wants no part of it: disjointing and hacking and slicing the flesh of steers and chickens is not to his taste, he's been to school, he'll go to work in an office in clean clothes that don't have the sickly smell of blood and the reek of burnt chicken feathers clinging to them. The younger son wants to become a player of baseball—what can you do? America! Liebowitz is getting on in years, his health is not what it should be. That the business he made should not end with him, that it should give when he dies a little capital to his grandchildren, he wants to take in a partner. If in the process he can also do a deed of charity to be written beside his name in God's book, so much the better. From a poor man he does not expect money. But for the right man, a man of skill, a man who can keep his customers happy, he will pay a good wage, and take out of it every month a portion towards the purchase of a partnership.

It is the chance of a lifetime. Even with the portion paid for the partnership Aaron will earn almost twice what he makes on the loading dock, and at the same time he will lay the first stone in the foundation of the house he has dreamed of building, which is simply his sweet home and shop in Khashchavata just as they

# Richard Slotkin

were, the image of wife and children in the calm stillness of amber, translated to the clean safe spaces of America. He seizes the deal with both hands, writes to Sarah to prepare herself, that it will not be long now, and crosses the bridge to Brooklyn.

The streets in Williamsburg are broader than on the Lower East Side, they let the sun spread itself across the plate-glass front of Liebowitz's store and illuminate the display of naked chickens hanging by their necks from steel hooks. The customers look more prosperous, their cheeks shine, their clothes are clean. Aaron appears in their midst like the ghost at a feast, in his long black coat with patched sleeves hanging on his lean shoulders, his full beard ragged with unclipped ends, smelling of the ghetto—garlic, sweat, filth. He must be made presentable—Liebowitz takes him in hand. He'll have a room to himself behind the store, with a water closet. There's a bath-house two blocks away—that he should make use of it! New clothes must be found—Liebowitz's hand-me-downs are so far above his own things that Aaron begins to feel like a gentleman. The beard must go—Liebowitz's round cheeks are clean-shaved, this is Brooklyn not Khashchavata.

These are the terms on which good fortune comes to him. He accepts, by stages, first the beard trimmed, then shrunk to a triangular chin-piece, and finally all gone but the mustache. His face feels strangely cool and clean, his body (washed and steamed once a week at the bathhouse) in its new American clothes feels strangely alive and healthy.

He has charm still—a skilled, good-humored man in the prime of life. So on one day and the next a young widow, an unmarried spinster, will throw him a look of the eye, you know the look.

He knows men who have forgotten the wives they left in Russia and married themselves an American woman.

When the thought of such a man occurs to him he brings the cleaver down *whap!* and splits a rib-roast into chops.

And yet he's a man, in full health—you understand?—and for

32

# Greenhorns

years his nights had begun with the tumbling pleasures of his wife's body with his own. Now for . . . two years? Three it was already!—the whole time of it suddenly rushes past him like a black wind. . . .

A long time, a long time to live like cheder-boy. It is unhealthy to live that way. Strange thoughts mounted to a man's head, and his flesh did not sit right on his bones. And there were women—they were a familiar sight on the East Side and easy enough to find in Williamsburg—swaying down the street with powdered cheeks and lip-rouge, leaning out of windows, a wink and a nod, a smile, sometimes a little shamefaced, sometimes gay, as if to say it would be good to have a little fun, why not? Polish and Italian women of course, but Jewish women too.

But at the end of the day he always says no. His dream is to tumble with his own wife in the same bed that remembered all their pleasure. To put another woman in that bed would corrupt and erase what he most desired in life. That Sarah should come to him and begin their life again!

Then her letter comes: not a word in response to his good news, he can't tell if she has even received his letters. Her words, written down by the scribe just as they fell from her mouth, are scattered, frantic, there's a pogrom in Mogilev, the army is ransacking the countryside for Jews to feed to the war, it's not safe to move, Grozner's store is gone, she has no work, they won't take the boys they're too young but they took every man in the next town, he must come back, he must come for them and take them away with him. . . .

He has become invisible to her. She cannot see, has no idea of who and where and what he is, and what he has to do to get them out. How can he come for them? Even if he could get into the country, they'd only grab him for the war. There was nothing to do, nothing but put his nickels together and buy them out of that sinkhole.

But what about himself? Could he see *her* any longer? That image of her and the boys fixed in warm amber light—it had no relation to her letter, the frantic rushing desperation of it, the fear . . . and they must be hungry too, no meat from the store, no money coming in, on what was she feeding Yoisef, and Chaim, and Binyamin?

And here he sits with his belly full, his clean healthy flesh wrapped in clean American clothes, his face shaved, his prosperity accumulating week by week in Liebowitz's account book.

But what else should he do, dress in sackcloth and starve himself? To save them he needs money, and this work earns money faster than any other. But to do it he has also to dress himself well and keep himself presentable. He has nearly enough for their passage, but he must also see to it that they have what to live on when they get here. What good will it do them if he lives on husks and makes himself wretched and sick?

He looks sideways at his reflection in the mirror and scorns his own reasoning: "As long as you're healthy you can always hang yourself."

That winter Russia lost the war with Japan and revolution exploded across the country, strikes and riots, events tumbling on each other, no man could make sense of them. In February 1905 the Tsar promised reform, then for Passover loosed the Black Hundreds to massacre Jews in Zhitomir and Odessa and a hundred towns across the Pale. The heart that might have grieved for the suffering of his people could feel nothing but the horrible single terror of *what was happening to her, where was she*, she and their children with her, all of them becoming invisible, a fading photograph.

Every Sunday he haunts the rooms of the *landsmanshaft* and the offices of the Jewish refugee agencies, but no word comes from Khashchavata, and by no means can money be delivered to any of the towns in that region. He is hanging between two worlds, living in neither. Sarah's words come back on him like a curse, *With one ass he sits in shul and goes to the fair*: his ass in Brooklyn, six days a week behind the counter *khacking* meat with his cleaver and giving the *reggeleh kustumeh* his smiling charm, because a man has to live and what else is he to do?—and every night his soul goes flying a hundred thousand miles over steel-gray water and empty space and Germany and Poland to his little town and his house . . . and just as he is about to land there it comes to him that he does not know if any of it exists any longer on the face of the earth, for all he knows the house is burned the town flattened, Sarah and Yoisef and Chaim and Binyamin hacked like cuts of meat and fed to the dogs.

In December 1905 he finally puts every cent he can find together, throws in the money he has put toward the partnership and borrows the rest from Liebowitz, buys a money order and sends it to be forwarded to her through a bank maintained by a refugee agency in Berlin—an organization funded by Schiffs and Rothschilds and by the pennies of shirtwaist makers and pushcart peddlers, which cared for Jews fleeing across the Polish-German border and strove to make contact with communities in the zone of riot and massacre.

Everything he had and expected to have was out on the table— if he lost now his pockets were empty, he could do nothing more for himself or for those he loved, his life and theirs would blow away in the wind.

The agency got the money, but could not find a way to get word or cash to one Sarah Rubinow in Khashchavata, Mogilev Guberniya, through a Russia that was ripping itself to shreds. The crisis stretched out into the next year, not a crisis but a situation, a way of life, Reds and Cossacks fighting in the big cities, strikers with clubs and peasants with sickles and pruning hooks storming the police station at one end of the town and massacring the Jews at the other—and what the mobs and the Black Hundreds let live the typhus and the black cholera devoured.

Until at last at the end of March 1906 a paper came from the agency, and was passed to him through the Khashchavata Society: is Aaron Rubin of Brooklyn the same person as Aharon ben Yoisef Rubinow, husband of Sarah? She wishes it known that she is in Vilna with her child.

# Richard Slotkin

Yes he is, of course he is that same man, who else would he be! But how is it possible, by what unimaginable epic of wandering and misfortune has she gone from Khaschavata to Vilna, she and her child.

Her *child*? There are three children, the agency in Berlin is making a fatal error and is deaf to explanations made by transatlantic cable. In a fever of anxiety he finally begs the great men at the offices of the *Kehillah*, the council of New York's organized Jewry, to help him explain that enough money must be transferred from the agency in Berlin to Vilna to pay the passage for Sarah Rubinow and three sons—*three* he insists, Yoisef, Chaim, Binyamin.

In the end it was done. And the day came.

December 1906 and a chilly spitting rain when he crossed on the Ellis Island ferry and waited on the dock for them to come walking out of the castle. There was a crowd that day and he scanned the faces as they filed out, some skipping or running, others shlepping along, greenhorns all of them, *Italienish, Poilish*, a frightened scurrying woman in a shaitl and her husband with earlocks, an old woman in a black babushka and shapeless sack of a coat dragging a four-year old, eyes on the ground as if afraid it will open beneath her. She looks up as she passes him and their eyes catch.

"Ay Gott," he said and his heart jumped.

The woman? She saw an American gentleman, terribly clean and neat like the doctor who examined her in the castle, a goy in a suit-coat and tie with a small mustache. . . and eyes that catch hers and are suddenly terrified.

And by that, in the blink of an eye, she knew him and she didn't know him.

"It's you," his mouth said, but not as if he willed it. He looked down at the child clinging fearful to the coat that hung on her, and a smile sprang up in him, ". . . and the little Chaim. . . ."

She almost laughed at him! The idiot, to mistake Binyamin for Chaim! As if the black *kholeria* would give up its dead, as if

36

the child had grown no older in the endless years since the man left us!

But then in the next breath she saw him swallow in its bitterness all the meaning of his mistake, and in that moment she almost pitied him, and remembered that after all she knew him very well. Without believing it in her heart she said, "So, I'm here. So."

They stepped together and put arms around, they were two grown people, they knew what was to be done in such a moment.

But when the strange man went to embrace the child, the little boy's face closed like a fist.

So it had come to him as Yankel prophesied. He went to make his family a place in America, and that he achieved. But to do it he had made a great hole in his life, in their life, a hole empty with vast miles and years of absence. Now when he looked in her eyes he saw the depth of that absence.

And she? She remembered how once she had seen her children and her grandchildren in his eyes—but now when she looked she saw eyes that had never even seen her little man Yoisef with his serious face, seen her Chaimeleh with his silly clever ways, burning and shitting with cholera until they were dead and shut up with worms in the dirt *they should rest in peace*, and Aaron nowhere, a void, an emptiness—no one but herself to ask over and over what kind of God was it who would turn the rules of life upside down and kill the older children with their mouths full of words, and leave the baby bawling and whining? But she would never tell Aaron the whole story—he had no portion in it.

They would live with that emptiness. They were not children or dreamers. In this world you either make a life or let the wind blow you into your grave. They were husband and wife. Children were taken from them? With God's help they'd make more. Their house and store devoured? They'd sweat and strive and build them up again.

# Richard Slotkin

But not as it was. *Farlorene yorn iz erger vi verlorene gelt*, lost years are worse than lost money.

At the card table he draws a card and Manny says, "You went to the market—did you buy the hen?"

"What I went to get, I got." But he's failed to fill his flush.

He had bet everything he had in life to win his family safe to America, and in winning he lost. Let the sages unravel it! But how could he have done better? Even Moses could not persuade God in His infinite mercy to spare a single Jew of those that fled with him from Egypt. Aaron Rubin had saved two of four. If he'd stayed they'd have grabbed him for the army and fed him to the Japs, and then who would have rescued his remnant from the Black Hundreds?

For years he'd asked himself, *what if he'd sent for them from Bremen, wouldn't Yoisef and Chaim have been spared the kholeria that killed them?* Now the thought makes his blood freeze—today they'd all be sitting together in a room waiting for the Nazis to kick down the door and slaughter them like cattle and hang their carcasses on meat hooks.

No. He had made the great gamble, and won what there was to win: a life in America where except for these mornings at the card table he lives as a stranger, his words fall on ears that hear only English, he's living in a country of the deaf. And the truth is that he feels like a foreigner in his own house.

Berel echoes his thought: "So how are your children?"

"Making their way in the world, thank God . . . by their own strength." It's a formula of words which he believes is somehow transparent to men but opaque to God, who must not understand that he resents his children, because if you curse the luck God sends you He's liable to send you worse.

Binyamin remains a stranger to him. It took Aaron months to get used to the fact that he was *Binyamin* and not Chaim, and years later he'd slip and call him "Baby," as if he was still the youngest son—when in fact he became the oldest as Sarah bore him Michael and Ida and Jake. But then, these American children didn't belong to him the way Yoisef and Chaim did, they would not be his Kaddish and keep his name alive in his own town. Even Binyamin had become American, "Ben" as he liked to be called, refusing to admit he'd been born on the Other Side.

He has to admit that these American children did all right for themselves. They walked away with his luck in their pockets—and that's fine, that's just what he bargained for, to nail himself into the floor like a board that they should step on his head as they strolled out the door. His disappointment is that his *nakhes*, his joy and pride in children, should come from these Americans and not the ones for whom he had risked everything—and won! But also lost. The ones he buried . . . or no, left behind for his wife to bury and himself to never see again, or her young years, or that look in her eyes.

You can't win back yesterday's day.

Except that when he plays cards there are moments when he feels a wild hope, that—if he puts himself in the way of receiving it—his luck will come back to him; that a miraculous combination of cards will show that God still has an eye for him, that if he is not yet David the King still he is one of the Chosen, not a tree without roots to dry up and wither in the air.

And if that wonderful combination should appear, then what? Nothing much: only it would prove that his life was justified—that he hadn't spent his years and his children and the love of his youth like a fool.

So he looks at his hand and sees what he sees. "One card," he says and makes his play.

# The Other Side

My wife's people and mine came from a dozen different *shtetls* scattered across eastern Poland, White Russia and the western Ukraine. It might be possible, through diligent research, to establish just where these towns existed, some for centuries, until each and all were wiped so utterly out that it was as if they had never existed.

When I was growing up the names of those places were rarely mentioned. It was said that so-and-so had been born "on the Other Side," and when I was a child that was how I thought of where we came from: a place totally Other, whose nature was not to be described, only known through doubtful hints of decay, of shame, of contagious disease, of an all-encompassing malevolence.

My father's eldest brother lied about his birthdate, not for vanity of age but because he didn't want people to know he was born on the Other Side.

The old zeydehs came from there—not really grandfathers to living families, just ancient, ruined-looking old men, perched like a row of buzzards on a bench outside the *shul* on the High Holidays, cackling in Yiddish, rubbing snuff on their sore gums and offering you a pinch, holding out the tin in broken fingers.

In 1948, when I was six, my Uncle Abe's "baby brother" appeared, a Displaced Person straight from the Other Side: a forty-year-old man with a shy sweet smile and the bloodless incurved look of someone in remission from cancer. His visit was brief. He had to go to Montreal, Canada; the American government wouldn't let him stay. Maybe they thought what he had was catching. He wept when he had to leave: Something in the country he'd left behind had devoured every last vestige of family that remained to him, leaving only the American brother, with whom he was not permitted to stay.

Cousin Bella was different. She was born on the Other Side, but in her that heritage took the form of a charming accent, a European manner, and the kind of deep and serious devotion to the arts we associate with Russian intellectuals. She was my wife's father's cousin, a small woman with bright brown eyes. We met in 1968, when she was in her late sixties—she was as old as the century—and after that we saw her about once a year, usually at a wedding or bar mitzvah.

The large hall would be filled with people laughing and yelling hello, enjoying with high drama the family news while the brass and accordion combo rollicked with practiced enthusiasm through *Tzena Tzena Tzena*. There'd be a long table where swans of ice overlooked the display of cold cuts and smoked fish and rye bread rounds, watermelon-bowl fruit salad and franks-in-a-blanket and mounds of chopped liver. In a room full of boisterous hugs and lipsmacking kisses she would give you her little hand in greeting, and lean in for a peck on each cheek. That makes her sound cold, but hers was a European courtesy. There was real warmth in her look, and real pleasure in the little smile she gave you. When she spoke her accent was more Russian than Yiddish, with that rising/falling musicality and the slightly drawn-out vowel sounds. She was always impeccably well-dressed in tones of gray. Her makeup was very simple—a little face powder, touches of rouge on the cheeks.

Her eyes lit up when I told her I studied American literature. She had discovered a fellow spirit, who read great works with the serious attention they deserved. She loved the Russian novelists, and the Yiddishists Isaac Peretz and both the Singers, I. J. and Isaac

# Richard Slotkin

Bashevis. In English her tastes were narrower, but she was devoted to Dickens and Shakespeare—she would not miss a performance of Shakespeare if tickets were to be had! American writers she did not know well enough for a serious appreciation. Perhaps Hemingway? Her smile was ironic, as much a comment on her own ignorance as on poor Hemingway. But I must tell her which Americans were worth reading—I was a scholar, she would welcome my opinion.

She lived with her husband in an expensive co-op near Lincoln Center. They had tickets for everything—the opera, the ballet, the Philharmonic, the chamber music series. "It's heaven to me," she said without any irony at all. She had played—no, she had *studied* piano as a girl in Russia. Her father had been a merchant in a small town outside of Bobruysk, a liberal man who had had ambitions for his daughter that exceeded the traditions of the *shtetl*. He paid for tutors in Russian and mathematics and music, and with determination and patience and the necessary payment of bribes had circumvented the quota system that barred Jews and won her a coveted place in the *gymnasium*, the Russian high school that was the path to university. She had spent two or three years in *gymnasium*, which fed her intellectuality and gave her voice its Russian lilt.

Her husband was cut from coarser cloth: a craggy-faced giant with a shock of white hair, like a Jewish Carl Sandburg, except that his expression was bashful rather than prophetic. He stooped a little, a very large gentle man trying not to scare the children with his size and barrel-organ voice. His education had stopped before high school, but he could keep in his head the accounts of a successful dry cleaning business, which he grew from a single steamy shop—his wife and he sweating over the machines, the air thick with naphtha and the smell of steam-ironing—into a franchised business with stores all over the northeast.

Whatever their differences they were a real married couple. They went together to the plays and ballets and operas and concerts. At first he went because this was something she loved, as well as something improving, another way to better himself. But her feeling was infectious. By the time I met them he was as deeply into it all as she was. Their difference now was that she preferred concerts, he the opera. She would lift an eyebrow when he went on about Donizetti and Verdi—"the sentimental murderers, the coloratura mad-women!"—and then "forgive" him.

He would hulk shyly behind his bright small wife, gazing down at her with a look on his face that seemed to be wondering, *By what luck, by what grace had he come to be married to this Pauline Kael, this Peggy Guggenheim, fallen from a higher sphere?* Her affection for him had a wry turn, but that was just her style—as if a part of her stood away from anything she said or felt. The affection was real. When she looked at him it was with the admiration and trust that a kindly giant deserves.

They had two daughters. Both were educated and accomplished women, but they always seemed a little in awe of their mother, who, after all, had never actually graduated *gymnasium*, and had been for most of their childhood the wife of a hardworking shopkeeper. Perhaps it was a reaction to her grand manner. But she had another quality that was less conventionally intimidating. It was the darker side of that ironic style that played through her conversation— again, as if part of her stood away from anything she said or felt. Despite her engagement with the moment and the people around her, there was a Watcher behind the sparkle of her eyes, whose nature was so strange that from its viewpoint everything in the opera or ballet, everything in the bright bar-mitzvah or wedding-world, was seen askew or aslant. It would be frightening for any child to see that strangeness in her mother's eyes.

But at some point the mother did reveal herself to her daughters. One of them told me the story at an anniversary party some years after her mother's death.

That wonderful manner of hers was her father's gift. If now she entered a room as the one everyone had been waiting for, it was because that was how her father had looked at her. Benish Krakower was a widower, the owner of a kind of general store in their little town outside of Bobruysk—in the Pale of Settlement, the western districts of the Empire in which the Czar required his Jews live, and not elsewhere under penalty of law. It was a *shtetl* devoted to the unchanging rigors of *torah* and *halakhah*, worshippers drawn away from the grievance and despair of their lives by the appealing world-blindness of Hasidism, chanting the phrases of the Law in loud unison to deafen their ears against a universe of menaces and enemies. All the fathers asked—and they prayed for it passionately—was "a Kaddish," a son to say the prayer for the dead for them when they were gone.

In that pious town Benish Krakower was exceptional for his mind as well as his prosperity: a *misnagid*, a man of the Enlightenment, of Reason and Progress. The last prayer he ever uttered was that his wife should not be killed by the child-birth that killed her. After that he did without. To live was hard enough without wasting time and breath on what was of no avail. The world was as it was—take it from there. He had no sentimentality—an iron head. But a heart to feel he did have. The iron head told him the child was innocent of the mother's death. The heart loved Bella entirely—more than loved, rejoiced in Bella.

Let the orthodox pray for sons: Bella was all the Kaddish her father ever wanted, and he would give her everything—and more—that a Jew of that town would want for his son. Only she would not study Torah, but secular subjects so she could pass the examinations for *gymnasium*. He wanted for her, not simply wealth, but the education that would allow her to live life as nearly as possible as she would have it, a life of powers and pleasures. Let it be music or mathematics, the concert stage or engineering, whatever was her will. She was her father's wildest hope, a defiance to the Gentiles and an affront to the pious.

So her father did whatever was necessary, accepting without hesitation the rigid logic of the order that shaped and distorted Jewish life in the Pale: labored and saved for her tutors, abased

# Greenhorns

himself before school officials, ate his fill of Russian shit, stooped to bribery when that was what it took, that she might have what she deserved. And he won—she won—she went to *gymnasium* and prospered there, and came home for school vacations with her head full of poetry and philosophy, visions of enlightenment and progress. More than that: while others would leave their visions and polemics in the coffee house, for Bella if an idea had value she must live it. She was a socialist—pious fathers had been known to sit *shiva* for Red children, but her father trusted her vision and courage. Such courage he himself had not dreamed of having, but he was proud to see it in her, and was a little in awe of her.

Then the Revolution swept through Kiev. With a bunch of her fellow students she joined what was not yet the Red Army, marching and making propaganda. A man with a hat and boots, therefore an officer, sent her out with two or three other Jews and a ragtag unit of displaced factory workers and demoralized soldiers to rally her village. The muddy streets were hysterical with fear, and she and her comrades tried to calm them. The leader of her detachment and his commissar spoke of democracy and the working class, of a Russia which would no longer know Jew from Gentile—ideas so foreign to the lives of that town that they were without meaning.

Then it was her turn to speak. She wore a uniform jacket looted from the barracks of a military school, a pistol on a leather belt—pale face under a furious mass of auburn hair. Her father was in the crowd, his look filling her with confidence. She spoke not as an agitator but as a native of that place, naming things her people could actually imagine hoping for: a government respectful of their dignity and their rights, that would let them live and earn a living safe from the malice of their neighbors, that would listen to their pleas with sympathy and understanding. When she was done the silence was serious—it was clear she had given the crowd an earful and what to think about. Some wild youths even gave a cheer for the Revolution. She was eighteen.

That night she ate supper with her father. Benish Krakower

# 45

was terribly proud of his daughter, and terribly afraid for her—impossible to untangle one terror from the other. The world was falling apart around them. In that chaos his daughter stood out, shining for all to see, her voice clear and sharp where her comrades were muddy and indistinguishable from each other. He was full of forebodings, but he was also proud of her. He trusted in her strength. The proof of that trust was that he delivered himself of his fears truly and unstintingly, along with every warning he could imagine, and in the next breath gave her all the encouragement she needed and deserved, and left it to her to balance the fear and the aspiration.

In the morning she went back to where her unit was billeted in the little police station, and everyone seemed suddenly doubtful and confused. Their leader, who wore stolen officer's boots and a policeman's tunic, had had three messages during the night: he must go here, and there, and the other place, none of which had any relation to each other, and no reasons given. But that they should go was plain enough. Something was up.

*What happens to the village if we go?*

Shrug. *They'll be safer without us.*

So she said goodbye to her father, who was sad that she had to go, and still anxious for her—but maybe also a little relieved that her "army" was being careful with her life. She marched out of town with her cadre, down the road to where they camped in a wood. For that departure she never forgave herself.

Because after they left the Whites came to town—she heard the shooting and screaming and saw the smoke. She wanted her unit to go back but the commander found twenty ways to say *what good would it do*, and her friends held her when she tried to go herself.

So it wasn't till two days later, after the Whites had gone storming off to strike the Red forces defending Kiev, that she got back to the town. The houses had been broken and burnt down, the muddy streets were full of smashed furniture and shit-fouled featherbeds and shattered crockery.

# Greenhorns

She found her father lying in the road in front of his house—the house half burnt, half collapsed. Her father was lying in the mud where they had beaten him to a pulp, and stamped his face with their boots, and castrated him and cut off his penis and ground it into the mud next to him. And him still breathing, bubbling blood at his nostrils.

A black knife divided her soul and she became two different people. One was a scream of grief and horror, a loved and exalted daughter-child facing the tortured and ruined and degraded body of her father, whose thoughtful kindness had always and forever nurtured her—and all around her the wreck of everything she loved and everything her life had been and every dream of what her life was intended to be.

And the other Bella was an iron heart and a cold eye, which saw all of that ruin, and accepted it simply because it was there, and this was now the world. She would be kind, as he was kind, but it was the cold eye that allowed her to see exactly what *kindness* must be in such a time and place, and the iron heart that empowered her to use that knowledge, in the face of cruelty and wreckage and disgrace.

With her small hands she picked up what was cut from him, so that he should be buried whole, and she threw her coat over him so that if he became aware he should not think that she had seen his nakedness and shame. She dragged him over the sill of his ruined house and into a room with three ruptured walls and a piece of ceiling.

He woke up and saw her and groaned, *Ay tochterl, you must not see me* and gestured at his body.

"I haven't seen you, Papa" she said. "I just got here. Shmuel the Sexton covered you and brought you inside." The lie was safe, because Shmuel himself was no longer among the living.

Did he believe her or not? He sighed and did not speak again. She sat by him in the broken room for three days and nights, now and then wetting his lips with water to tempt him to drink. If she spoke to him, she never told anyone what she said.

# Richard Slotkin

She still had the pistol, but she didn't use it.

When he was dead she went out into the yard and scraped a trench with a board and dragged him to it, wrapped in the coat. She threw her military jacket over him, piled earth on him, and stone rubble from the house, and fragments of furniture and boards. She said Kaddish: *Yisgadal v'yiskadash, sh'may rabboh.* . . .

"The end of our life," she added.

And yet one lives.

So she joined the long march of refugees east and south away from the fighting, across the shelterless plains and the frozen Dneister River, to Bucharest where she sold the pistol and where the *landsleit* of her little town had set up an agency; to America, and the dank tiled halls of Ellis Island; to the giant husband who looked like Carl Sandburg, to the shop and the daughters, to the Lincoln Center.

# Honor

My father was smoke and my mother was fire. They fought bitterly all the years I knew them. He was a man proud of his success in business and of his standing in our little town of Bershifkeh, and he seemed to be fearless. She was an angry frightened woman for whom the world was all meanness and terror. Yet she was the one with the cold eye, who knew that cash was better than credit and weakness was shame. For her he was—and always had been—a *luftmensch*, full of illusions.

In my memory of him, and of our life on the Other Side, my father was a great man, a broker in wheat who dealt with high and low, honored throughout our district as one whose word was as good as money. But she was right that he wasn't fit to deal with America. Some people, America takes them green and makes them over a new person, smart and strong. Not my father. He was a greenhorn when we got off the boat, and stayed green until the day he died. America didn't fix him, it finished him off. The boys I ran with in Brooklyn—Izzy and Peshky, Nate and Ruvn—would have called him a chump if I had told the truth about him. Which I would never.

As for my mother: she had ferocity, and hardness to deal with a hard world. Yet she also stayed a greenhorn, never learned the language, saw everything—friends, enemies, hopes, fears—as if we still lived in Bershifkeh and not in Brooklyn Williamsburg. Over there she knew where the lines were drawn, Jews on one side and everyone else on the other. But America was gangsters and grifters, and everywhere from every side greedy people, Gentiles and Jews alike, after you for a buck. Here she saw *everyone* as an enemy, and no one to trust, so she was left with only anger and her own strength. Which weren't enough.

So it was left to me to make our place in America.

## 1

Bershifkeh was a little town out in the plains one day's ride from Kiev. I know it was one day because when I was four I broke my leg, and the bonesetter set it crooked. So my father took me to Kiev to a real doctor to have it broken again and re-set.

It was winter, so he wrapped me in a blanket and I sat next to him on the seat of our horse cart. When it came down sleet my father opened his black overcoat and sat me on his lap and closed his coat around me because I was very small. So we rode like that, and I smelled his smell of tobacco and sweat, and I felt his arms when he hupped the reins to make the horse go.

I remember that the bone-breaking hurt, both times. But my father told me the broken leg would grow stronger than the other, and his words came true.

Our *shtetl* was dropped like a handful of stones in a gently rolling ocean of wheat. The wheat flowed out as far as you could see to the north and west, rippling and flashing in the sun when the wind passed over it, a green ocean in the spring, an ocean of polished gold by summer's end. On the east and south the ocean was blocked by the low black line of a forest. That forest was a *finsternish*, a black nothing full of black birds. Some hidden thing would stir them and make them all lift off at once, and it looked like the forest was *reaching* for us.

Everyone lived from the wheat. When the crop and the price were good everyone lived well. If the crop failed or the price dropped everyone suffered, Jews and peasants alike. The peasants grew the wheat. Jews couldn't own land in that district, so they made harness and clothing and lamps for the peasants, and sold things out of shops, and they were brokers for marketing the grain.

My father was such a broker, an important man in our little town.

In the summer he would ride round the district to talk with the landed peasants and the stewards on the big estates, to look at the golden fields and judge the yield for himself. Sometimes he would take me with him, riding in that same horse-cart. He called it our *britsky*, which is a kind of carriage for rich people to trot around the town. But ours was really just a small wagon with a canvas cover stretched on a frame of hoop-poles that the peasant Ivan Pavlich made for my father.

Poppa wore a round black velour hat with a broad brim, a long black coat with his white collar showing at the top. His cheeks were pink from riding in the open air. He had a thick full black beard, and when he smiled his white teeth flashed. He would call out in a strong voice, like the barker of a circus coming to town, "A good day to you, Ivan Ivanovich," if it was a peasant, or "*Gospodin* Pavlichenko" if it was a landlord's steward. "And to you, Avram Isakovitch" they would answer, smiling and nodding to seem agreeable, though some would spit to one side before giving him greeting—but he never took notice of it. Yet sometimes a peasant would come out into the yard with his wife following, carrying a platter on which were a loaf of bread and a dish of salt.

When they were agreed on a price they would shout, "Good!" The peasant would spit in his hand, my father would spit in his, they would clap hands together and give them one hard shake and the deal was done. There was never a paper signed with any of them. He told me: "A man who keeps his word, and gives you good value for your trade, will never lack for business."

He would never lack for business, because everyone knew his word was good. He was a man of honor. If he promised the merchants to deliver wheat at a certain cost, he delivered it. If he promised the peasants such a return, he saw to it they were paid. He made the same price for peasants as for the landlords—so he was known among the peasants as an honest broker and a good Jew. Even *muzhiks* who spat when he came in their yard kept faith with him if they shook his hand.

We were not rich, but in that town we counted as well-off. Most people paid for milk with potatoes, but we always had some cash money to spend, and for father to give to the poor at Yom Kippur. We had a pew in the Wheat Brokers' Synagogue, which was built with money raised by my father and the other brokers. It stood right on the muddy market square in the center of Bershifkeh. The wheat brokers all sat in pews at the front near the *bima*, and their wives in the front of the women's section. When we all prayed together you could hear my father's voice ringing out above the rest, a rich baritone, with as many curls and lilts in his singing as if he himself was the cantor.

My mother was a little woman, like a sparrow with a sharp beak, and she would peck at him as he sat at the table in the evening, drinking his tea and smoking a cigarette and reading his newspaper. Her litany: *Why live lean when other brokers live fat?* They would skim off a little of the earnest money, or pocket a gift of rubles from the buyers for persuading the peasants to take a lower price. They took care of their own first, and let the peasants take care of themselves, Jew-haters that they were.

Till he'd look up at her and say: "A man who cheats is a shame before Jews and goyim alike. Better to starve than to eat such shame." Then he'd make a circle with his hand, "We live well enough." And he'd smile a satisfied smile.

In 1909, the year after I was born, there was a pogrom in my mother's old town and her brother Benny escaped from it with just his skin and the clothes on his back. My father offered to take him into the business, but he wanted nothing more to do with Russia. So my father gave him clothes, and money for a boat ticket to America, steerage class.

My mother said, "Sell out and let's go with him," but my father said no. He didn't think they traded wheat in New York, and even if they did, how could he do business where he knew neither merchant nor peasant? In Bershifkeh his word was good with the *muzhiks*, the landlords, the merchants—everyone.

She spat. "These people look at us like a dog looks at meat. One day they will set their teeth in us, no matter what words are between you. In America at least they let you live."

My father shook his head and shrugged and grinned with all his white teeth, like an actor in a play, as if to say: *women will talk, what can you do?* "Shush *mameleh*," he said soothingly, "I know my business. I'm not a *luftmensch* like Benny, to throw away my trade and take a jump in the air, dreaming I'll land in a golden street. You'll see: he'll beg his bread in America."

At first it seemed my father was right. Benny sent back letters, he was working like a machine making shirtwaists and couldn't save anything. But then after a while it seemed he was doing better, and he'd send my mother little presents of money.

Which annoyed my father—did the man think we needed charity?

Because that year, which was 1914, my father made a lot of money—the country was mobilizing for war and the price of wheat went up. That winter he leased an orchard from one of the big landlords. A Jew couldn't own land in that district, there was nothing that belonged to us, but that year we lived like landowners. In the spring, when the black twisted limbs were thick with white and pink blossoms, we rode there in the britsky, and he'd sit on the ground with his back against a tree-trunk and smoke a cigarette and drink up the orchard with his eyes. "Go," he told me, "play and enjoy yourself. All these trees are yours," although in truth they were only rented. Once I climbed into the limbs above him and shook the branches so that the blossoms fell all around him like snow, and he looked up at me and laughed at the joke.

Later when the trees gave their fruit we had piles of cherries and pears, fresh and sweet, and my mother baked pies, and cooked the fruit with sugar and put it in jars, and dried some in the sun on white cloth, and all the next year we ate the sweet preserves and the dried fruit.

## 2

But that next year was bad, and the year after was terrible, and the next worse still. The war ate up the young men in the district. There weren't enough hands, even with the peasant women and girls working, to make the kind of crops that were wanted. What wheat there was, the landlords and peasants hoarded. In the fourth winter of the war the Tsar disappeared, and the woods were so full of bandits and young men escaping the army that you couldn't get the wheat to market anyway. For a while there were Germans racing all over the countryside on trains that bristled with cannons and machine guns, stealing the wheat from the granaries and sending it back to Germany. Then the Germans went away and we heard there was a revolution in Kiev.

The wheat ocean turned blue-green that spring, then bright gold as the summer burned its way toward September. My father kept driving from farm to farm, but he could not get a handshake. There was talk that the Red government would buy the whole crop at a high price, but also that because they were Reds they would seize it and give it away. Poppa put our savings in a pottery jar and buried it under the horse stall, except for little purses of ready money which he hid here and there around the house.

On the last day, I remember he had to go away—someone said there was a man at the depot, buying wheat for the Red government in Kiev. Mother said, "A man who isn't there is buying wheat the peasants here won't sell you," but what else was he to do? He got in the britsky and drove away.

She looked at me. "We can't live on air," she said. She took a leather purse out of her apron and put some coins in my hand. "Go up to Silenko's. His wife said she'd sell us a hen." Silenko was a peasant whose little farm was just outside town.

# Greenhorns

The beaten path ran between solid walls of golden wheat higher than the height of a full-grown man. Silenko's farm was at the top of a rise, a low house with one window behind a yard of stamped earth. I called hello from the gate, but there was no sound or movement from the house. Empty.

Something stirred the air behind me. I turned and looked back. From the rise I could see over the wheat, which hid the rolling of the earth in a plush golden coat. Beyond the town to the east I saw the solid black wall of the forest, and as I watched the black seemed to swell and lift itself up and burst, a million black birds flying out and up over the blue sky.

My feet froze to the ground. I thought of running to Silenko's house and banging his door to let me in, but the house was a dead man's face with one eye.

I looked back toward the town. I heard loud popping sounds and shrill faint cries, and then smoke came up in a sudden cloud from the middle of the house-rooves. In one thought I told myself *I must run home and save Momma I must run home and Momma will save me*, and I started to run back down the dusty slot between the high walls of wheat.

I heard the thump of horse-hooves from around the turn ahead, but because of the wheat I was blind. A man ran out of the wheat around the bend, the breath ripping out of him *khaah! khaah!*—it was Reb Kalman the tanner. And then in a swift black rush horse and rider burst out of the bend behind Reb Kalman at a gallop, the rider's arm swung up and long steel flashed above the white hair and red face of the rider and as he came on top of Reb Kalman his arm scythed down and flashed *thump* and Reb Kalman bowled over himself in the dust. The rider pulled his horse back on its tail, its back legs skidded in the dust and it kicked the air in front.

Then the rider saw me.

The horseman whirled his arm, I saw his sword bright and sharp above his red face and white head as he slammed his heels into the horse and leaped out at me.

# Richard Slotkin

I turned and dove into the wheat on the left-hand side of the road, smashing down the stalks, pushing them aside, and then I thought *He's high up, he'll see the wheat moving*, so I threw myself down to the side, and tried to crawl deeper and deeper among the close-planted rows carefully so the wheat would not give me away. Then I stopped moving and pressed myself flat flat, made myself into the earth, no difference, I wasn't there. I heard the horseman yelling *Fucking Yid Pig Bastard!* the horse blowing and thumping, and the *thresh! thresh!* of his sword slashing against the grain as he searched me out.

The sword-sound stopped and I heard the Cossack cursing to himself, and the horse shuffling its feet as he stood in place, and its whuffing breaths.

Then the sound of the horse walking away.

I slithered after them to the edge of the road. The Cossack had dismounted and stood over the body of Reb Kalman. He reached into his pants, pulled out his cock, and pissed on Reb Kalman's body. He laughed the way a dog barks.

I writhed my way backward into the wheat till I couldn't see the road any more. I heard the sound of the Cossack riding away back toward the town. I stayed hidden in the earth until the air began to darken, then crawled out and started to sneak my way home.

Smoke was boiling and boiling up into the dusk from where the town was, lit with fire from below, and I smelled burning wood and burning meat. It seemed that everything was turning to smoke, maybe even Momma and my father were turning, if I couldn't get back to them I myself would float away alone in the sky like a flake of ash.

At the first house you see going into that town there was a woman lying face-down in the road. Her house was burning. By its light I could see that her head had broken open and pieces of raw greasy meat were spilled out of it. So I ran away off the road and went all around the outside of the town to the bottom of the slope below our house, and crept back up to the horse-stall in our back yard. There were no lights in our windows and the thatch roof was smoldering, a smelly dirty smoke drifting up against the moon.

She called me from the stable, a whispered yell harsh and urgent, and I ran into the hay-sweet darkness and she grabbed me hard and I grabbed her. Then she thrust me away and gave me a shake that made my teeth rattle: "Where did you go what did do you are you trying to kill me?" I tried to say what happened, how the man on the horse chased me and I hid in the wheat, but she just glared at me with terrible eyes, and kept shaking me and yelling that I was trying to kill her. "But I brought you back the money," I said and held it out to her.

She slapped my hands away and the coins flashed and fell on the stall floor. She slapped my face—but then grabbed her head with a loud cry, and ran to scrabble after the coins in the hay. "We're all going to be killed," she said, "we have to get away from here!"

"Wait till Poppa gets back!" I cried, "he'll know what to do!"

She gave a crazy laugh, "He'll shake them by the hand, and the hand will cut our throats!"

I crawled into the hay and covered myself with it. No, I told myself, they'd never catch Poppa, he'd whip the horse and race away from them. He'd come back, and he'd stop Momma being angry-crazy, and we'd get in the britsky and he'd drive us away from here, to where we'd be safe. In the end I slept and woke up hearing his voice but not believing it, but this time it was really true.

He was standing at the entrance of the stable holding my mother's two hands in his. He had been on his way back from the depot when he saw the smoke and heard the shooting far away, and without a second thought drove straight to Ivan Pavlich's, a peasant but a man you could trust—all the years he had done business with him! Ivan Pavlich said of course he would hide him in the barn. But he'd have to leave the horse and wagon when he left—it was too dangerous to travel on the road. Ivan would bring the wagon to their house the next day without fail, upon his sacred honor, and in my mind I saw them spit in their palms, and clap their hands together and shake.

"And you take the word of that *muzhik*?"

"He hid me in his barn!" He paused. "And I gave him a purse of money . . . all I had with me."

"Good! So now he'll come for the rest of it! So you'll let him walk away with our last kopeck!"

"He gave me his word."

"*Yid*, that was his word, *dirty yid* was his word for you. . . ."

"Enough," he said. "You shame me in front of my son. To ridicule a man is worse than to kill him."

And that was it, she stopped, *enough*.


We waited that night in the horse-stall for Ivan Pavlich to come get us. When it was full light my father slipped out to go look for him, and I followed. Of course it was more dangerous outside, but to me it was safer to be where he was.

We peered around the corner of a house into the main street. It was littered with smashed furniture and heaps of wood and cloth, but no Jews—only peasants were there, stumbling in and out of the houses and up and down the street, yelling to each other and carrying away our feather beds and cradles and chairs and chests and boxes and long bolts of cloth and bags of flour and potatoes. I had a friend, David, whose house was right across the way, and in front of David's house was our britsky. Then Ivan Pavlich came out of David's house with a pile of coats and blankets stacked in his arms, which he dumped in the back of the cart and turned right around and went back in for more.

So now I knew that Ivan Pavlich was not going to drive us away from there in our britsky.

When we got back to the horse-stall Poppa said nothing about Ivan Pavlich. Only that the bandits had burned the wagon and shot the horse.

I didn't say anything, If I told her what I saw she might go angry-crazy again and I was afraid of that. I wondered if maybe Poppa was afraid of the same thing, because to ridicule a man before his son is worse than to kill him, and that's why he didn't tell her the truth.

But then I told myself *No*: he did it to save his strength so he could carry us out this place.

## 3

I remember that we walked for days and it was raining. There was a long line of Jews from our town and others in the district. We followed the railroad tracks to a city, Vinnitsa I think, and hid from the rain in the corners of derailed freight cars. We had to buy food, the Russians demanded double and triple prices and our money drained away.

Word came to us there that there was a Jewish Agency in Bucharest, Zionists and people from the Jews in America, and if you could get there they would take care of you. So all of us got up and walked away into the distance.

Summer became fall, the rain became sleet. Sometimes my father carried me. The sleet became snow. We came to a river and it was ice from one side to the other, but the people in a long curling line were walking across it. We followed them. It was night. I remember how cold and empty and black was the air above the flat floor of ice.

## 4

On the outskirts of Bucharest a line of soldiers and police stopped us. With them were men from the Jewish refugee organizations, and they led us to a shanty-camp just across the river from the city. There were many different organizations there, Zionists, the Jewish Agency, the American Committee, and agents for dozens of *landsmanshaften*. We just called them "the Agency." They set up shop in an old warehouse just outside the camp, and every family went to register with them.

Three clean clean-shaved men, wearing suits and white collars and ties, sat behind a row of empty crates that served for desks.

# Richard Slotkin

They had piles of papers in front of them. At one end an armed guard with a Zionist armband stood by a strong box from which they would take small packets of money. We shuffled slowly forward closer to the desks. As each man stepped up to the front, a man at the desk would ask what was his name, and who was with him, and what town was he from. Then the man at the desk would hand out a packet and mutter something to the other men by the table and they would make marks in black-bound ledger books.

When it was our turn my father strode up to the desk. "*Gospodin*," he said, "good day to you," and he held out his open palm for the handshake, the way he used to do with the peasants and the stewards of the big estates. But the man at the desk didn't see, he was looking at his papers. My father stood there with his hand out. The man asked him what his name was, in a Yiddish that was like German. My father told him and he wrote it down; and then, still writing, how many in your family; and then, where are you from, Bershifkeh. And all the time Poppa is standing with his open palm displayed before him. Finally the man lifted his head and looked at us, and without another word picked a packet of money out of the chest and slapped it into my father's open palm, then looked down and wrote again in his ledger. My father stood there looking at the top of the man's head until the people behind us grumbled, so then he moved away.

I looked up to see his face. He looked strange—like a man dazed by a blow. In the hard clear winter light I noticed that grey hairs were spreading from his mouth and nose out into the black of his beard, as if his breath was a frost.

We were safe for the time. We learned that the Bershifkeh *landsmanshaft*, the society of people from our town who had gone to America, were paying the Agency to find people from the *shtetl*. Money was being raised in small batches by the society, and by individual families. And a wealthy man named Kovelson, who had moved to America twenty years before, was sending large drafts of

# Greenhorns

money to bring their townsfolk and kinsmen to the other side. But until the Agency sent our names to the *landsleit*, and the *landsleit* sent the money for our passage, we had to live on the little the Agency was able to dole out.

We lived outside the city in a hole with boards over it. There were hundreds of us there, waiting. Twice a week my father would go down to the Agency to get a little packet of money and ask whether word had come for us from America. But the word didn't come and the money was not enough to live on. Once or twice my father tried going back between the pay-days, but he came back empty-handed and with burning cheeks.

So my mother and the other women from the camp would go to beg bread in the town. But Father refused. "We're not beggars! To beg money is a shame before Jews *and* goyim alike."

"Of course we're not beggars! We're brokers in wheat!" she sneered. "So go find yourself a peasant, and get his crop to market, and bring me a fistful of rubles to put food on the table."

He looked at her with contempt, crossed his arms, and sat down on the little stool that was set in front of our little hole in the ground.

"Cross your arms like that when I serve the kasha! At least go talk to the Agency and wring a few coins out of their miserable pockets."

His eyes pinched as if a pain went through him. But he grinned, showed her his teeth, a bitter smile for all to see, and said, loud enough for everyone to hear, "Go, make a beggar of yourself, you should live and be well."

My mother laughed at him, and walked away with the other women.

He watched her go, sitting straight-backed on his stool like a man on horseback, glaring sternly left and right.

She's wrong, I said to myself, we don't need him to go beg. Better he should stay here and guard our goods, a job for the strong man not the weak woman. To prove he was right I decided I would go out and get us food or money without begging.

61

# Richard Slotkin

The camp was full of boys roaming around, looking into every-thing. There was a dump outside town and we ran over there in a mob, dozens of us, and scrambled over the piles of crap, looking for food, or for things you could trade like a battered pot or kettle, and we'd yell if we found something as if it was a game, and then everybody would come running to that spot and pile in and tear the garbage apart, and then the big boys would show up, throw the little ones aside and take everything.

I was afraid of the big ones, but I was also furious with my need, not just to get food or money but to prove She was wrong. I remembered the Cossack. I found a strip of metal like a piece torn from a tin roof—that was my sword. I gripped it my hand and when I saw them mobbing around a pile of junk I went for them, cursing the way my mother would have cursed them and waving the metal strip around my head and slashing with it like a man crazy with anger. After that they left me alone in my part of the rubbish pile.

I found there a rusty cast-iron kettle with no handle and some pieces of kitchenware. On my way back through the shanty-town women called out to me, *where was I going with that pot, what would I take for it?*

I remembered my father bargaining with the peasants, and I did as he would have done. *Well what will you give? So much? But maybe the woman across the way would give more!* With a wink and a nod and a shake of the hand I came away with twenty kopecks.

When I came back that night my parents were sitting around our little fire on boxes, hunched over. She looked so miserable, my mother, that to cheer her up I ran to her and took her hand and opened it, and opened my fist and let the kopecks clink into her hand.

My father raised up and saw, and he grabbed the coins from her hand. "What's this?" and his face furious, never had I seen him angry before, and at *me*! "A *schnorrer*," he cried, "begging money in the street! A shame on me before the goyim *and* the Jews!"

# Greenhorns

My little mother jumped up and I thought she would strike him, but her fists froze before her and they shook. "A shame?" she said, "A shame on you and not on him, at least he brings us what to live with!"

He glared at her, as if he was going to say something fierce. But then his eyes widened and lost focus. He seemed to shrink down. "The Agency . . . I can't keep asking them for more," he whispered, "they treat me like a beggar."

"And what else are you?" she said in bitterness.

If they had let me get a word in, I could have squared myself with both of them: because I hadn't begged the money, I had fought for it like a Cossack and bargained for it like a broker. But between my father's pride and my mother's ferocity I could not squeeze a word.

## 5

Finally, toward the end of winter, the Agency sent for us. Money had come from America, and some of it was from the Bershifkeh *landsmanshaft*. There were long lines in front of the desks, and a lot of discussion as to which fund a given family was allowed to draw on.

We shuffled slowly forward till we came to the desk and the tables, and there were the clean-clothed clean-shaved men sitting in chairs in their suits and white collars and ties. What's your name and how many with you and what *shtetl* are you from, and the men would make marks in their ledgers as they handed out the little packets of papers and tickets and money from their different boxes. My father kept clenching and unclenching his fists and stamping his feet, grinding his teeth to keep his mouth shut, and his fear caught me up like a fever, my heart was jumping, I was afraid they would run out of papers before we got there. And your name and how many and where are you from, your name and how many and on and on and by the time we got to the desk my father's fists were closed and his lips split in a nasty grin and his teeth were clamped together. He cried out, "Why do you make us linger in suffering till you give what belongs to us!"

At this the man at the desk looked up. "Ah," he said, "Our oldest and most valued customer."

My father's face became swollen and red and his eyes bulged.

"Well Avrum," said the man, "today you're in luck—money from America and a second-class cabin on the boat." He lifted an envelope out of the box before him and one of the other men passed him a packet of paper money out of a different box. He held them out but my father still stood with his fists clenched at his sides.

"With my own money," he said, "with my own money I bought my wife's brother a steerage ticket to America. If the goyim didn't burn my house and steal my money. . . ."

The man at the desk gave a weary shrug and let his eyelids droop. "Look," he said, "let's not quarrel. You've had a rough time of it, but your *landsleit* remembered you—so here's your ticket to the Golden Land. Second class! You'll live like princes, in a cabin with beds."

"I don't want second class . . . I don't want first. Give me tickets for steerage."

The man at the desk let his jaw drop open. "Are you crazy? Are you trying to make trouble for me?"

"Second class is charity! Steerage I bought my wife's brother. Steerage I could buy with my own money if they didn't steal it!"

The air around us was bubbling, people laughing, people calling out *Idiot* and *Don't be crazy* and *What's he doing?* and *Stop holding up the line!*

The man at the desk gave him a *look*, his mouth wrung up to one side. "You've got your head twisted around."

"*Ich fyf on dir*," my father said, *I whistle on you, you're ridiculous, you have no more substance than the air.*

"All right! You want steerage, I'll give you steerage," and the man picked a different set of papers out of his box and put the first ones back.

# Greenhorns

I felt something go slack in my father's body, I saw his fist open a little and lift as if beginning to reach out. "And the difference in money. . . ?" my father said.

The man blew a breath out of his mouth. "Look, we have a fund to give tickets and a fund to give money. All I have is tickets. If you don't want the second-class that's not. . . ."

"So you put the difference in your pocket!" my father cried.

The man just shook his head, and turned to the man next to him. "What do you know—he saw right through me! That I came from New York to this anti-Semitic pest-hole to make my fortune." He waved us away and beckoned the next man forward.

My father turned on his heel, and with his back straight marched away through the murmuring and outcries of the people waiting in line and I followed him. My father was a broker in wheat, an important man in our little town, and not a beggar to make us ashamed before the goyim and the Jews.

When my mother found out she banged her head with her fists, "Are you crazy? Are you possessed? Do you mean to destroy us?"

But she hadn't been there, she didn't see the man at the desk, she didn't know that Poppa had to keep us from being shamed before the whole world as beggars and charity cases. I was there, I saw, I understood.

Yet it was hard to feel good about it with my mother glaring at him, refusing to listen or believe. He still held himself straight, but he seemed smaller, as if the meat was withering on his bones. The white hairs from his mouth had spread through his whole beard. I noticed that one corner of his beard turned yellow from the cigarette smoke, and when he showed his teeth there was a bright amber spot where he sucked in the smoke. Also he would cough when he smoked, not a bad cough, just a sort of soft dry cough.

## 6

Before they let us on the boat they took us to a bathhouse and steamed our clothes to kill the lice, and then we washed. Then we tramped up a gangway into the iron ship. There was a hole in the deck and we went down it, down steep metal steps to a lower level, and then another lower, and another, till we got to the steerage. It was a big room with steel walls and ceiling, rows and rows of wooden tiers of bunks lining the walls and in the middle a series of tables and benches screwed to the floor. A man in a dirty white jacket led us to our place, which was the middle section in a three-level tier of bunks, one crackling mattress for the three of us to share, with a family of four below us and another of three above—and the same stacks of three in rows all up and down both sides of the room.

There was a crowd of people in there, maybe a hundred and fifty, and the only air came through a pipe in the roof and the one door at one end of the room. The space filled with the smell of breath and sweat, and the stink of unwiped asses and babies' shit, and babies crying, and always a fight going on, or someone groaning or coughing—some of it bad, lung-ripping coughs—and after the boat left the harbor and the floor began to throw itself up and drop itself down there was the smell of vomit and the bark and rasp of people khawking their guts out into buckets. The floor rattled from the engines below, and bitter fumes of the oil they used also spread among us. We slept in that and we ate our food in it, weak soup or stew ladled out of iron kettles, sodden lumps of bread, meat that had an acid edge. My parents wouldn't eat it anyway, it wasn't kosher, so they and the other Jews lived on pickled herring and bread and tea.

But the fish was disgusting to me—look smell taste all vile. Let them eat it if they can't do any better! Me, I slipped away and got in line with the goyim, Russians and Ukrainians running from the Revolution, Greeks escaping from the Turks—and got a bowl of stew or a plate of meat and potatoes, tucked myself in a nook behind a row of bunks and ate my fill. My parents were too miserable to notice what I was doing.

# Greenhorns

## 7

When we got to America there was a great cry in the steerage and everyone grabbed their little bundles and rushed to get up the staircase. We poured up into a penned-in space of deck, the crowd so thick that the ones in back couldn't force their way to the railing, so all they saw of America was a wall of overcoats or the back of someone's head.

On the deck above us the people in the second class were pointing and shouting. There was a giant statue in the harbor, there were tall buildings! I worked my way through to the railing, but all I could see on my side of the boat was a big wide brick building with a fancy tower on it, and behind it a low wall of smokey buildings that I thought was the City. It looked no better than Bucharest. This was Ellis Island, and Jersey City squatting behind it.

On the deck above us we saw men in uniforms talking to the second-class passengers, and gradually the crowd up there thinned out. Later we found out that the immigration officers came to those passengers in their cabins, checked their papers and passed them, so when we filed down one gangway again onto the stone path to the great brick building, they filed down another and right out to where a ferry was waiting to take them to the City.

When I turned to watch the ferry I saw New York for the first time, the buildings like a range of mountains shooting into the sky, unbelievable.

Then the brick building took us in, long tiled corridors smelling of medicine and a great high tiled room full of benches and booming with echoes. They hung tags on us, and we shuffled down long lines, and policemen that were doctors looked in our eyes and made us open our mouths, and pinched us, and made remarks.

That night we were let out and the ferry carried us across the dark water to the mountains that now had a million lights in them, each light a window, rows and rows of windows rising level by level up into the sky, and behind each window there were people living lives. My mother's brother Benny and his family were waiting for us on the dock, they ran into us with a bump and there was hugging and crying, they had been so frightened when the second-class passengers got off and we weren't there, they had paid the Bershifkeh *landsmanshaft* for second-class tickets for us. Benny had chased one official after another till he found out where we were . . . what happened, did someone steal our tickets?

We rode in streetcars through the City and across a great bridge, till we got to the tall house in Brooklyn where Benny's family had their apartment. Inside it was warm and bright. Everyone was talking at once, and crying.

Benny was telling everyone to sit down so we could eat. "Take off the hat and coat," he said to my father. Benny had on a light brown jacket that fit his shoulders and ribs, and a white shirt with a bowtie, and his wife wore a bright colored dress that was soft and flowed when she moved. My father was wearing a square black wool coat that hung to his knees and a round velour hat with a wide brim, the nap worn off. I had the same hat—the crown stuffed with paper because it was a little big for me. My mother wrapped her head in a scarf with fringe hanging down, and wore a wool coat that stood out around her body like a bell. Our clothes also breathed a stink into the air, the ghost of steerage.

"First thing tomorrow," said Benny, "we burn those clothes— all new we got for you, you'll look just like Americans!"

My mother was smiling and nodding like she couldn't wait, and it was fine with me. I was hungry as a horse and felt like an idiot with that hat on my head. I looked at my father and saw him straighten his body a little and make his face smooth and empty.

Then Benny took us upstairs to the apartment they rented for us. I looked out a window—I was way up in the air, it was like being a bird, the space below me seemed to suck at my belly in a way that scared me and tickled me at the same time. Our house in Bershifkeh was right down on the ground—I had never been this high in the air before, not even when I climbed the tree in the orchard my father

leased, and shook the flowers down on him and he laughed. I heard
Benny laughing, "What privy?" he said, "in America you do your
business in a room of the house," and he showed us where the crapper was at the end of the hall.

In our apartment we had two bedrooms, a sitting room, a kitch-
en with a coal stove, and a room with a sink and bathtub—"and
that's to wash yourself in, Avrum—not to store your coal!"

"I know what's a bath tub," my father said, but Benny went on
laughing. He had a good nature, Benny. My mother was proud of
him, "Look what he made of himself all those years while we laid
in the dirt in Russia waiting for that vermin to come and rob us."

That got my father's goat: "Who bought him his ticket?" he
said.

"A steerage ticket," she answered, and he was silent.

## 8

A Jew doesn't starve among Jews. The Bershifkeh *landsmanshaft*
did what it could to help the refugees establish themselves in New
York. They found factory jobs for those that used to be workers
or craftsmen on the Other Side. But my father had been a wheat
broker, a businessman. For him Kovelson, the rich man, found a
grocery store a few blocks away, and gave him a little capital to
stock and run it.

At first I helped my father in the store. It was a small place,
not more than fifteen feet from side to side and maybe twenty front
to back, with behind that a smelly store-room and a booth with a
crapper and sink. The front door was on one side, and the rest of the
front was a big glass window, with painted letters that said Grocery
in English, Yiddish, and Italian. There were shelves along one side
wall and across the back, piled with cans and boxes of food and
soap and cereal, and on the other side a marble counter that my father sat behind all day. There were electric lights, but it was always
dark in there, except in the morning when there was sun through
the glass window. My father didn't like to keep all the lights turned

on if there was nobody looking at what was on the shelves, so he just left the one on where he was by the counter, and it was a weak bulb—he used to tilt his Jewish paper toward the window to read.

There was a chill up your back if you sat behind the counter, because on the wall behind was the meat-box where he kept salami and kosher sausages and cured meat, and the dairy-box where he had jugs of milk and butter and blocks of cheese, and under each of them was a big block of ice that the ice-man brought every day. My father could take a piece of salami out of the meat-box behind him and cut it right there on the counter, or cheese. Or a sour pickle—he had a barrel of pickles that you could smell all over the store. But the chill wasn't good for him. He kept coughing the way he started on the boat, a hard dry bark, but sometimes it went on too long. He sat there all day smoking cigarettes one after the other, waiting, reading his paper.

If someone came in he would stand up behind his counter and give them his teeth, a big smile again, and in the poor light you didn't notice the amber stain of the cigarettes. He still wore his black coat from the Other Side and the round hat with the wide brim. He'd say "Hello, good day to you sir, good day to you madame," and then if they just stood there he'd bustle around and turn on the lights for them. The customers were Jews from all over Russia and Poland, but mainly Italians that lived in the neighborhood. They'd pick out their goods and bring them to the counter and pay him the money, which he counted and put in an iron box. Or if they didn't have money with them he would write what they owed in a black ledger book, and shake hands across the counter. So I knew he was himself again, doing business in the way he always had.

I remember one time an Italian woman put her goods down on the counter, looked in her purse, and became very upset, *ay-ay!* making a prayer with her hands, rocking herself from side to side. She had no money, her husband took her purse, they didn't pay him this week, not even a crust of bread in the house! My father talked gently with her, she became calm—then he reached across and they shook hands, and the woman was very happy and took her packages and went without leaving money. "She will pay me later," he said, and wrote it in the ledger.

But I had a bad feeling about that one. In Russia, when two men smacked their hands together they grinned, like men enjoying themselves. This woman, when she walked away had a look that was sly. And it occurred to me that perhaps Brooklyn was not Bershifkeh.

If I could have stayed with him . . . but it was the law that I had to go to the American school, so I left him there.

## 9

It was a new world for me. In our street and in our school there were kids from all over, Italians and Irish and Chinese as well as Jews. My Yiddish could get me only so far. I had to pick up English in the street the same as I had Russian—but whose English, the Italians or the Irish or the Chinese or the Jews?

School was no help. The teachers were all Irish or German, they neither spoke nor understood Yiddish, so at the start I couldn't talk to them, not even to ask to go to the bathroom. Even though I was almost twelve they stuck me in a class with the littlest ones, jammed into a desk and chair combination that was made for a baby. When we stood in line or went outside for recess I looked ridiculous, chest shoulders and head over everyone else. In the schoolyard they let me know it, called me dummy and rock-head and *analfabett'* and *farshtoptener kopf.*

I was walking down the halls, trying to find my classroom, when something hit me bang in the back and knocked me sprawling. A big fat face glared down at me, crazy eyes, red lips and a mouth bulging with teeth. "Get out of my way!" he yelled, and gave me a kick for good measure.

The other kids just kept walking by, but one stooped and gave me a hand up, a skinny boy with a mop of black hair. "That's

'Q-Balls,'" he said. "Don't get in his way." Then he moved on. That was as far as anyone's kindness went in that place.

In the schoolyard at recess I was alone, leaning against the fence while the others ran and screamed, tagging each other and running away, yelling "It!" and "Base!" and god knew what else. Across the yard the bigger kids hung together in a bunch, laughing and punching each other in the arm. Q-Balls' fat blond face grinned out of the middle of the pack. I was afraid of that face, as if it was the Cossack with the white hair.

I slid over into a corner and sat on the ground. My mother had made me a sandwich of cold meat for my lunch, in a brown paper bag. I was wondering whether now was the time to open it and have a bite, when suddenly there was Q-Balls leering down at me. He gave me a smack on the side of my head and snatched the bag out of my hand. "Hey lookit!" he yelled, and waved it over his head as he walked away from me.

In my head I felt, *that food is all I have to myself* and I hated Q-Balls like death but also I wanted to cry. Then I thought what my mother would say, crazy-angry she would shake me, *what kind of lump what kind of weakling are you to let that bastard take what belongs to you*? In that moment the fear and the hatred both together swarmed up out of my guts like the black birds boiling up out of that *finsternish* forest in Russia, and I got up and ran like a crazy person and slammed into Q-Balls from the back so he stumbled forward and sprawled flat on his face. I scrambled up his back and grabbed him by the hair behind his head and tried to twist his head off like Momma did killing chickens.

The next I knew he had rolled over and thrown me off and was sitting on my chest punching at my face, which I twisted away from him, but he still popped my nose so it bled, and made my cheek swell.

Somebody pulled him away off me.

Then the same wiry black-haired kid who had stooped to me in the hall was bending over to give me a hand up. "I gotta hand it to you," he said, "you got more *kishkes* than you got brains." He was maybe a year older than I was. Izzy, he said his name was.

Three other boys were gathered around Izzy, and they all looked me over. "Whaddaya mean brains," said one of them, "this is the chump they put in with first-grade."

Izzy punched him in the arm. "Lay off! You were a greenhorn too when you started out."

He spat in his hand and stuck it out to me. "Give as good you get, or die trying, that's the way!" I spat in my hand and we shook. And then the same with the rest of the gang, Peshky, Nate, and Ruvn. A pact of honor, just like it used to be between my father and the peasants and the merchants.

So even though I got a bloody nose and a black eye, jumping Q-Balls was lucky for me. If I hadn't done it, so far as Izzy and the boys were concerned I would just be another greenhorn chump. Now I was one of them, and we would stand up for each other.

My mother flashed her anger when I came home with my black eye and swollen cheek, and I told her how my lunch had been stolen. But when I told her that I'd fought Q-Balls to get it back she opened her eyes in surprise, and gave me half of a smile. "At least you fought back," she said. "Better you should *win* next time. But at least you fought."

For once she approved me more than my father did. "Tsha!" he said, making small of the fight. "There's always a bad element. You keep away from them. To brawl like a *muzhik* is a shame before God and man."

But there was no avoiding bad elements in America any more than in Russia. To live among people is to live with bad elements. What you need is people you can trust to help you deal with them. All that year, whenever we were out in the schoolyard, Izzy and the boys would gather around me; and when Q-Balls made a move in our direction we'd turn all five of us together, *We see you coming, we've got our eye on you.*

It was Izzy's idea that we should whisper to each other as he passed, and laugh like there was a secret joke. "That'll scare him worse than anything—us laughing at him. What do we have up our sleeve that we could look at him and laugh?"

To mock and ridicule a man, my Poppa used to say—it was worse than to kill him. But till America, who knew that mockery could be my own weapon, as well as the next man's?

## 10

After that things at school went well for me. I had an ear and an eye, I learned to read English and work numbers, and soon enough I was put into a class with kids my own age. My mother acted as if she expected nothing else. "I told you your brains would catch up with you." Then we recognized the sound of my father's feet, pounding up the stairs one step at a time, and her mouth pulled tight. "Not like him," she said. "Your father doesn't live in this world."

He held to the old ways, insisted that I go the *cheder*, to study Torah when I wasn't in school. But I had no patience for all the rules, eat with the right hand wipe your ass with the left, the rote and reciting, zimzimzim, zumzumzum.

In the street and the school I had a shining life. With Izzy and the rest I did everything, stole fruit from the fruit stand, sold newspapers, pitched pennies against an alley wall, carried betting slips for the numbers players at the barber shop. We were smart, we made a nickel here and a dime there, you can go to the movies, you can get bleachers for a Dodgers game. We were true to our word, we watched out for each other and gave as good as we got, or took our lumps for trying. In America whatever you can get away with is yours.

My mother knew the tricks I got up to. I think she was proud that I was smart enough to break the rules and get away with it, but she never said anything, to me or to my father. He would ask me about my school work, or the *cheder*, and nothing else—as if that was all the life he could imagine me living.

# Greenhorns

Izzy's father was an organizer for the Garment Workers. One Sunday the workers all went on a picnic and Izzy took me along. We rode the trolleys to a big green park where we cooked food on open fires and sang songs, and the fathers and sons played baseball. My father would always sneer when he saw kids playing ball in the street, "Bums," he called them, silly games like that were for the *goyim*. A Jewish boy must live a serious life. . . .

But Izzy's dad showed me how to swing the bat, and lobbed the ball to me gently so even I could hit it with one awkward *hack*.

On the way home Izzy asked me, "So what does *your* father do?"

I thought of him sitting in the store, smoking like a fire, doing business with a handshake and no money coming in. Judge him by Izzy's standards and he was a chump—a greenhorn so green that everyone and his cousin could take advantage of him.

Instead of saying that, I thought of all the things I was proud of in him and that's what I told Izzy: how he was once a broker in wheat, and all the goyim in our district even the big landowners would only do business with him because he was a man of his word, a handshake and it was as good as done. And the year he gave us the wonderful orchard, the flowering trees, the heaps of fruit. And how he saved us in the pogrom, and guided us through the snow and ice, across frozen rivers, and would beg no bread and take no charity to get us to America.

I guess Izzy told his father what I said, and also the rest of the gang, and they told their fathers. And the fathers told the mothers, so the word came around.

It was a hot day, enough to fry your brains. All the windows were open, and the apartment doors propped open as well to coax a breath of air to come through, and the women were standing in the hallway talking. I was coming up the stairs and heard my mother, and then Mrs. Cohen saying, "So from what my Yakov says, that's some husband you got—a man of miracles, to get you out of that slaughterhouse."

75

"The miracle is he didn't get us killed," my mother answered.

"But a man that was a broker, he has a head for business! Now that he has his own store. . . ."

She made a spitting sound. "As if one dropped money down a hole! Nobody pays him, he can't fill the shelves . . . it's a good day if two people come in. When the last box is gone even they won't come. But you can't tell him anything. He just sits in the dark and smokes. If he was an Irish he'd drink himself into the grave. He's a Jew, so he'll smoke himself dead with his luckystrikes."

I backed down the stairs and out the door. I walked down the street to where the store was. The sun still roared above the rooves above me but the glass front of the store was shadowed, and the glass itself clouded with unwiped dust. In the darkened store I saw the little blob of dull light from the bulb above his head, and his blurry shape leaning on the counter. His round hat was on his head, and his gray beard lifted as he took a sip from his glass of tea. Then he put the glass down and sucked smoke from his cigarette, and the end of it burned. It got darker as I watched, which made the glow of light seem brighter, but his image was smeared by the dusty window and all I could see was the shadow of him lifting his glass of tea, and drinking the smoke from the burning cigarette.

## 11

It happened according to my mother's word. In three months he was too sick to leave his bed, in five he was dead.

The *landsmanshaft* paid for his funeral. My mother kept her face covered with a black veil all through the service. I stood up and said Kaddish for him. Then we went to sit *shiva* in the apartment, cloths draped over the mirrors, my mother and I sitting on wooden boxes. She had cut the collar of my shirt with a scissors, and pinned a black ribbon over my heart.

People were talking quietly about him, a pious man, a good Jew, he had no luck, he had no years. My mother began to shake, and then she burst out, "Don't talk about what you don't know! He was fool! Let him be dead! He refused to live in this world, so let him leave it! He would have taken his wife and child down with him—and for what? So he could strut like a peacock in his own mirror!"

"Stop it!" I screamed, "you didn't know. . . ," but then I stopped because I didn't know how to finish.

Everyone was trying to shush us and pat us and make us quiet, but my mother saw only me. "You should know what I know," she said. She got up and went to the bureau and took out a flat black ledger. "Here," she said, "this is his book where he wrote down what those Italienishers promised to pay him, the way a gypsy promises. Take it, go to their houses, tell them to pay you the money they owe your father."

Uncle Benny said "Anna, you can't, it's *shiva.* . . ."

She flipped her hand at him. "Let him go. He's no yeshiva boy—are you, my son?" She almost smiled. "Go," she said, "It will teach you how to mourn."

I knew it was her meanness to make me do it—to show me what a chump I was for thinking my father was such a great man. Well, he *was* a great man on the Other Side, a broker whose word was good anywhere in our province, who had leased for us that orchard of flowering trees and luxurious fruit. But even I could see that what made him great over there made him a chump in America—while my mother was the same ferocious angry bitch on both sides of the ocean.

But also she understood the meanness and cruelty of the world. And I knew that besides her own meanness, she gave me this errand to teach me to look at life with a cold eye—to harden my soul against the blows the world had waiting for me.

So I took the book and went. The names and addresses were all written down, very clear, and next to the name the amount they owed and when they borrowed it. I was a little uneasy walking on the Italian block, but no one bothered me. Maybe it was the black ribbon.

# Richard Slotkin

I walked up the stairs to the first apartment and knocked, and when they yelled who was it I told them.

A man opened the door a crack and looked out. He was big, with brown skin and black eyebrows. I told him who I was, and opened the book and showed him the page. He twisted his head back and yelled, "It's the Jew's kid, he wants his money."

"What Jew?" a woman yelled back.

"The greenhorn from the grocery! He just died!"

"Let me talk to him!" she yelled, as if to say *let me get my hands on him*, and she jerked the man back out of the door and there was her face, round and plain, with a kerchief over her hair, and I remembered her from that time in the store, how she said *ay-ay* and made a prayer with her hands that he should give her credit for a crust of bread. "Beat it!" she said, "We don't owe you nuttin!" and she flicked her fingers at me the way you flick an insect off your arm.

"But I saw you," I said, "I saw you shake hands with my father. . . ."

She pursed up her face like when you spit and flicked her fingers at me again. "Shake hands *va fongool*. This is America!" and she slammed the door.

I just stood there. The slam of the door seemed to hang there like hands clapped over my ears. I knew it would be the same or worse at every door I knocked on.

Then the door opened again, just a crack. The woman's face, frowning. She stuck her hand out—without thinking I reached mine to her and she dropped a bunch of coins in my palm. "That's for the dead," she said, and crossed herself, and shut the door. For the living she didn't give a shit, but she was afraid to offend the dead.

Okay, I thought, at least I would have that much to take back to my mother so she wouldn't scream at me.

And that made me feel ashamed, that I should take charity from an enemy, instead of demanding what I was owed. That I should be so afraid of a woman's tongue that I couldn't tell her the truth. The way my father was afraid.

# Greenhorns

I wondered what he would have done if he was still the man that he had been back in Bershifkeh, the man honored for being true to his word, who always gave you fair value and an even break. But in America they have no respect for a word. They never give you an even break. My mother was right about that, even if she didn't know what to do about it. But Izzy knew: You have to show your stuff. You have to make it stick. You have to give as good as you get or die trying.

I found in an alley a coffee cup with the handle broken off. I put the charity coins in the cup, and carried it back upstairs to the woman's apartment. I put it on the floor in front of her door, and pulled out my *schvantz* and pissed in the cup, and it made me laugh to do it, the way the Cossack laughed pissing on the dead body of Reb Kalman.

I knocked on the door, and walked away down the stairs. I had just reached the street door when I heard her outraged scream from the floor above me.

I sauntered off down the street. It was my street now. All the streets were mine.

# Milkman

In the summer we would all go to a bungalow colony on Long Island—our family and my mother's sister's family, five kids altogether, and my mother's parents, Essie and Hersh a.k.a. Bubby and Zeydeh. My dad and uncle were only with us on Saturday nights and Sundays. They were partners in a grocery store and you can't shut down a retail business just because school is out.

First thing after breakfast we'd all go to the beach. Bubby and Zeydeh would linger on the sand, now and then shooting an eye at the water and giving it a deprecating shrug of the shoulder—it was trying to sell them something and they weren't buying. We'd all plunge right in and start splashing and carrying on, and when we looked up later they'd be limping down the beach into the water, Bubby shaking a little from the Parkinson's, Zeydeh favoring one leg, wading in with excruciating steps as if they were walking on coals till they were in thigh deep. Then they'd splash a little water on their chests, and Zeydeh would cup water in his hands and drench his bald head, "Ay, ay, it's a *mekhayah!*" a pleasure, a delight.

Then they'd hobble back out of the water and up the beach to sit in the shade of the umbrella. Zeydeh would shake out his Yiddish newspaper, the *Forverts*, that my dad brought out from the City, and he'd read bits of it to Bubby. Every item was sure to remind them of something or someone, but their memories were always a little different, and every story was a ball bouncing back and forth between them as they worked out what really happened, and who really said what.

They also wrangled over the fine linguistic distinctions between one Yiddish or English word and another, as to which most precisely suited the person, the attitude, the dilemma of the story. They had both come over when they were teenagers, so their English was a small branch grafted onto a Yiddish tree. Zeydeh could read and speak both, but preferred to read Yiddish. Bubby had never gone to school on the Other Side, and only a year over here, so she could read a little in English but not at all in Yiddish. Zeydeh liked to tell her she was illiterate in two languages. Her answer was that his was a *shtetl* Yiddish, from some speck of a town way out in the country where they grew chickens—hers was from a real city, Bobruysk, where she was born.

I understood enough Yiddish to act as interpreter when an American word was required.

"Ahyh," Zeydeh said one day, "Look where Moishe Cohen just died in the *Forverts*!" He leaned over to show her in the paper where the death had occurred. "Moishe Cohen," he prodded, "that dentist. He gave our cousin Esther-maydl her American teeth that time."

She closed her eyes and nodded. "He was a dentist, he was a *mensch*," not just a *man*, but a fully human being.

The name Esther-maydl was strange to me. In Yiddish it meant "Esther-littlegirl."

Zeydeh laughed. "Everyone called her that because even when she was already a lady she was still a child. It was something in her head."

"She was a dopey," Bubby said firmly.

"Not a dopey," he answered, "she was a dummy."

A snort of contempt. "What do you call a dummy?"

"A person who can't think—who when she's a grown woman she thinks like a little girl."

"That's not a dummy. A dummy is a *stimme*—a person that

can't talk. Esther-maydl, she should rest in peace, could open her mouth, but what came out of it made no sense."

"By us, we called a person with no brains a dummy."

"By you?" she said. "By you out in the country. In Bobruysk, in the City, we called that a dope."

"To me a dope is *a shtik flaish mit oygn*," a piece of meat with eyes. "A dummy means you can't add two and two, but still you are among the living. That Esther-maydl was always lively, always happy—living in dreck the way she was, with *nothing*, but she'd laugh, and she'd smile. . . ."

"And not a tooth in her head, dressed up in dishrags, she's laughing and smiling. A dopey! But sweet. And a *gute neshuma*," Bubby shook her head, *a good soul*—a natural sweetness of spirit, deeper and more instinctive than the commonsense humanity of a *mensch*.

"Did I ever meet this Esther-maydl?" At our family gatherings my parents are always introducing me to dozens of cousins whose names and relationship to me I can never remember.

"No," said Zeydeh, "she died when you were a baby. And she wasn't really a cousin. We called her Cousin Esther because she used to live with us."

"Live with us." Bubby rolled her eyes. "We adopted her. This one," she tilted her head at Zeydeh, "got a bug in his head—from her father, Isaacson the *Milkhiger*."

"You call him the *Milkhiger*?" he reared back in mock outrage. "He wasn't just a milkman, he was a magician!"

She laughed and brushed off his outrage with a well-practiced flick of the hand. "He brought you milk in bottles on a wagon with a horse. In Bobruysk we called that a *milkhiger*." She winked at me. I could see this was one of those conversations they'd had so often that it had become a well-rehearsed comic routine.

His answer was a patronizing smile: "*And* he did magic tricks on the street corner. He taught me! Look," he said, and leaned over to me and pulled a coin out from behind my ear and flourished it. Of course I'd seen him palm it, but I gave him a "Wow" anyway.

# Greenhorns

But Bubby shook her head. "Hands you got like a suspender-maker, not a magician."

Zeydeh laughed. "But Isaacson and me, together we *made* a dollar."

This was the story:

Zeydeh had come over with his parents when he was thirteen. His mother had bad lungs and his father neither brains nor luck. They lived in a tenement basement off Hester Street, with one dirty window at the top of a wall, a gritty stone wall that every night would break out in a cold sweat. The father was lean and pale and walked with a bent back. He could spit out a little English but not enough to get by. Zeydeh, who was then a boy named Hershl, would go out with him to find work here and there, sweeping out a store or pushing racks of coats in the garment district or hoisting and hooking non-kosher beef carcasses from the trucks—a nickel and a dime, while the mother stayed in the basement coughing and spitting blood. One night he heard his father crying out, *Ayy! Ayy! Ayy!* and his mother was dead on their bare mattress, blue in the face with a trickle of blood from the corner of her mouth. A wave of people washed in and washed out again, the body vanished. The next day his father was gone as well and Hershl neither saw nor heard from him again. Disappeared!

"Like magic," Bubby said, and Zeydeh rolled his eyes.

So he lived in the basement, tried to earn a nickel the way his father taught him, and failed. One night he came back to find that the *landler* had moved a new family into the basement room. He argued for his right to the room and settled for the return of his blankets. Then he went to bed down in the coal bunker near the furnace at the other end of the basement.

He met the Milkhiger because he was stealing the bottles and blocks of cheese left at the doors of the upstairs apartments and the Milkhiger caught him at it.

"He grabs my arm to hold me there. 'What if I go to the cops?' he says.

# Richard Slotkin

"'Go, and God be with you,'" I answered him, because anything was an improvement from that way I was living.

"'What if I go to your parents?' he says.

"'You'll make a long trip,' I told him, 'and you won't come back.'

"He throws me an eye. 'Come work for me,' he says. 'You can help me carry the goods and clean up the horse.'

"'Why should I clean up your horse?'

"'You can't take out if you don't put in.'

"'From nothing you get nothing,' I told him, wise as I was.

"'You think so?' He reaches out *snap!* like that and pulls a boiled egg out of my ear. I stood there like a golem. He crumbles the shell off with one hand and gives it to me. 'Eat,' he says. 'You'll live in my house and eat my food, and if you work I'll pay you two bits a day.'"

The Milkman, whose name was Isaacson, lived in one of the better buildings on the Lower East Side, a five story house with four apartments on each floor. His wife was a big round woman who looked like she lived on milk and butter and cheese, and he had a little daughter, Esther, who was five at the time—a bright-faced happy child always singing to herself. "But that's what babies do, so I didn't think anything." The husband and wife slept in one room, the baby slept in a kind of large closet, and Hershl slept on a mattress on the floor in the living room. There was one crapper on their floor which they shared with the other apartments. On Sunday Mrs. Isaacson would boil a kettle of water on the coal stove and pour it into a big galvanized iron tub on the kitchen floor, and one after another they'd come in and take a bath.

Six days a week—not on the Sabbath—they would get up before four o'clock and in the chill grey light he and Isaacson would go down to the stables, humid air full of the fetid sweetness of horse shit and rotten hay, hitch Perele to the milk wagon and clop-clop down to the dairy on West 4th, where they loaded clinking caddies of milk bottles out of the wide door with its cold breath

# Greenhorns

of cheese and spoiled milk. Then with the sun prying the streets open they'd go house to house and door to door. "Isaacson taught me how to *do* a job—from the first to the last, and don't skip over in between. He never broke a bottle. If you ordered a quart with cream on top, that's what you got. And he would knock the door so the people should know to take in the milk in case some goniff like the way *I* was should come along and steal it. Always he was cheerful and friendly with his customers. He knew their names and their children, he remembered from one week to the next what he talked with them the last time. So when you did business with him, it was like *mishpokhah*."

Which has no exact translation because the relationship doesn't exist in English. It's like family, but includes all possible in-laws and cousins by marriage, and also honorary aunts and uncles and cousins—neighbors and friends of such long-standing and tried sympathy that no bar-mitzvah or wedding or funeral would be proper if it did not have a place for them.

"He was no family to me," Zeydeh said, "but he was my family *that* time." He looked far away, remembering.

When their rounds were done people would be crowding down into the street, the grownups off to work, the little kids out playing on the sidewalks and in the gutter, the mommas sitting on the stoops or hanging out the windows to watch over them. Isaacson would pick the corner of a busy street, lined with shops both sides and pushcarts along the sidewalk, the people packed in from one side to the other. He'd drop a big milk-crate face down alongside the wagon, hop up on it, and call out to the street, "Hey! Hi!" and start to do his magic tricks. He'd take a deck of cards and fan them and fold them this way and that, and make an ace pop out. He'd pull eggs out of his nose and handkerchiefs out of his ear. One person would see him and call out, and another would come over, and so on and on till there was a whole crowd of them, little kids standing in front with mouths open like baby birds, and the grownups behind them, "Oooh!" and "Ahhh!" and "Oyyh!" as he made live

85

pigeons disappear and poured water endlessly from a tiny flask. "I'd go around through the crowd with my hat turned upside down and the people would drop in money, whatever came to hand. And that way also we *made* a dollar." Zeydeh gave Bubby a look: "A *magiker* he was."

"And a *mensch*," she said.

"And a human being," he agreed. "I would help him prepare the tricks, and help him sometimes when he was doing them. He worked on the magic the same way he worked on the milk. He was careful, everything he did he did from the beginning right to the end, and nothing left over. From him I learned how to *do* a job. But the magic he couldn't teach me. You need quick light hands. I got hands like a mechanic."

So when Hersh was sixteen Isaacson wrote to his cousin in Baltimore, that worked in a suspender factory. "That was a skilled trade, you had to be an apprentice first, but the cousin took me on." The cousin was no Isaacson, but he taught Hersh the trade, got him into the union, and found him a job making leather suspenders, "And I *made* a dollar that time."

"Also I met your Bubby there." He grinned, she deprecated the event with raised eyebrows. "A Southern belle—that's why she has an accent like Scarlett O'Brien from the pictures."

"English I have an accent," she admitted, "Jewish I talk better than you."

"Because you grew up in Bobruysk, *ich vyse, ich vyse.*"

Years went by, and he lost touch with Isaacson. How do you write a letter, and in what language? People move, how do you know where to send it?

Eventually Essie and Hersh moved back to the Lower East Side, and one day on the street he saw a young woman—skinny and filthy, dressed in rags you would be ashamed to throw in the garbage, shoes tied up with string, what hair she had that wasn't falling out was a rat's nest, most of her teeth missing and what's left of them black, but she's smiling and singing a little song, *la-dee*

# Greenhorns

*la-dah la-dee*, and something in the song made Hersh look at her with both eyes. It was Isaacson's daughter. He went up to her, "Estherel! it's me, Hershl! What happened to you? What's the story?"

She smiled and said how happy she was to see him and it was a good day. He couldn't tell whether or not she remembered who he was, or was just smiling and being agreeable like a baby, you smile at her she smiles back. He hadn't seen her since she was eight years old, still sitting and singing to herself like she did when she was five, but at the time he didn't take notice of it—she was just the same she had always been. But for a grown woman to be that way? Must be something wrong! "A dummy!"

"A *dope.*"

Eventually he got the story from people on the street that knew her. Isaacson had died of a cancer. It took him slowly, so he had to give up the milk wagon and the horse, and by the time he died they had nothing left. Then the mother died of a *kholeria*, who knows what kind of plague, there was nothing to pay rent with and Esther wound up on the street, sleeping on a pile of sacking in a basement.

"So your Zeydeh brings her home with him, filthy, stinking, and jumping with bugs. And on top of that, a dope. He gets the *mitzvah*, I get to scrub her with brushes and wash the hair she has on top and the hair she has on bottom with coal-tar water. On her head the hair fell out in patches. So now we live in two rooms, the man, the wife, three babies and a great big dopey."

"But she was a help with the babies," he appealed to her. "She was a sweet person, and she could stop them fussing just picking them up and walking around, and singing to them, *lu-lu-lu*, and tell them stories about little children just like themselves who found ice cream and treasures and brand new shoes. She sewed little dresses for them. She had fine quick hands like her father, and her momma had taught her to sew when she was little . . . it was when she got older that her head stopped working. And always she wanted to help out. . . ."

"Help? This is her help. I tell her how to make soup. I give

# Richard Slotkin

her chicken and onions and carrots and greens, I show her to put water in the pot, I show her to light the stove. The water is boiling. I take her two hands, put them on the chicken, put the chicken in the pot. She smiles! Three teeth in her head, but she smiles! And so we make soup, and we eat it up, and the next time she goes to make the soup I come in and she's standing in the kitchen looking at the dead chicken like it's going to bite her." She grimaced. "Plus she was also a woman, even if she had a head like baby. She wanted a man. She looked at men like a cat looks at a fish. If you let her out alone in the street some low-life would get his hands on her."

Zeydeh shrugged. "What can you do? Isaacson gave me my life. I should let his daughter live like a rat and die in the street?" But what could he do for her but keep her alive? Isaacson had taught him how to make a dollar, how to do a job, how to live a life. But you couldn't teach this Esther anything. "Whatever she was, a dummy or a dopey, that's what she was, and you have to *do* something. Her father showed me: this is how you live a life. If you have *gornisht*, you give who needs it a *shtikele gornisht*." If you have nothing, you give one who needs it a piece of that nothing. "And sometimes in the world, you do a good deed and a blessing comes back to you."

"Like magic!" Bubby said.

"Exactly," he answered. "If you want back, you got to put in. That's what Isaacson said, and that's how it happened."

"For his good deeds all he got was a cancer."

"For his good deeds I was there to help his Esther. The mitzvah I did to her was the same as if it was to him. And anyway: even if a blessing would have saved him from the cancer, he'd have given it up so his daughter should have it."

She had to agree. That was the kind of man he was, Isaacson.

Zeydeh leaned forward and looked down at me: "But what is there to do for such a person as Esther-maydl? A woman with no brains, no hair, no teeth—nothing but a cheerful heart and a loving disposition and a good soul."

# Greenhorns

I had no idea.

But Zeydeh did. "One day this *Moskowitz* gets off the boat and opens his little store on Rivington Street. A greenhorn—but not the kind whose whole world is wrapped up in a bindle tied with string. He was from Lublin, and he brought over a capital from the business he ran there. A little man, like a fireplug with a round hat and a beard. A pious man, what they call 'a Jew for the whole year,' a widower forty years old who had buried his wife on the Other Side. His children too, so he had no one to say Kaddish when he's dead. His sister, an old maid, kept house for him. He had a nice way about him, a smile like a, like a. . . ."

"Like a *shmendrik*," said Bubby, meaning *like a simpleton*.

"A *shmendrik*? This is a man who ran a business on both sides of the ocean!"

"With only three words of English—hello, goodbye, and denksalot."

"He didn't need English, he had salesmen that spoke his English for him."

She had to concede. "Maybe not a *shmendrik*. I don't know what's the word in English . . . he steps into the street with his eyes open wide like a day at the circus."

"An innocent?" I offered, but the Yiddish word is *unshuldig*, which only means "not guilty."

"He was a *greenhorn*," said Zeydeh, "that's all you need to say—but the kind of greenhorn that stays a greenhorn till the day he dies. Every day with him was like Columbus. *A noyer velt,* a New World fresh at his doorstep every morning. Why not? Life was good to him. But he had also a *behnkn* . . . what's the word in English?"

"A longing," I told him, "a yearning."

"A longing. He was a married man without a wife. A father with no children. An empty heart is like an empty belly—a man has to fill it or die. So: *he* wants a woman for a wife . . . *I* have in my house one woman more than I need"—he clapped his hands: "A market!"

# Richard Slotkin

Bubby was shaking, whether from the Parkinson's or from laughing inside you couldn't tell. "So tell her how you sold him that piece of goods!"

"Moskowitz had in his head a full inventory of Yiddish, Russian and Polish. Till he could clear the shelves he could only take on a little English here and there. So he wanted an *American* woman, who could speak English and raise his children to be real Americans. Esther-maydl was perfect for him. What language she had was American. It was good enough to tell stories with, and if you told her to go ask the butcher for a fresh chicken she could go and ask the butcher for a fresh chicken."

Bubby: "What happened after she got it back to the kitchen was another matter."

He lifted a palm, *let there be peace between us.* "A true housekeeper she could never be," he conceded, "but she could sweep a floor and dust a table and use a needle and thread. She cared for children, and could keep them safe—the little ones loved her, it was a pleasure to watch her with them. Above all, she was a good soul. You could sift her for a year and not find a single crumb or speck of meanness. And she wanted a man . . . like a baby wants cake. When a woman looks at a man, savoring him with her eyes that way, he feels himself begin to shine like Thomas Edison."

Bubby: "But the man also has eyes to see what she looks like, with her six pieces of hair and her three teeth."

"Yes! Because of her looks, he wouldn't see the good of what she *is*. But! If you could make Esther-maydl look like an American girl—then you just set her in front of Moskowitz. He'll take one look and go hire the fiddler.

"So first she needs clothes—cut a picture from a magazine, get some bolts of cloth from the remnants store, add your Bubby and a Singer and we have the makings of a dress. Then shoes: I know a shoemaker that, if I make him a couple pair suspenders he'll make *her* a pair of button-up shoes. Then the hair—you couldn't grow her a new head to replace what fell out. So a wig. Moskowitz was

90

a pious Jew: if his American wife happens to wear a *sheitl* so much the better! But you can't just put a piece of old carpet on her head—this is an American girl, not the widow of some Hasid fresh out of Bialystok. A good wig can *cost* you a dollar—and I don't mean a dollar, I mean a *dollar*."

Bubby was shaking, and she leaned over and gave him a pinch on his arm. "So he stole the tail off the fruit man's horse!"

"It was your idea," he said in justification. "And it was a beautiful horse, with a beautiful black tail that the fruit man, the Italian, combed out every night and kept so clean and shiny. So I went in one night with my leather-shears and" a snip in the air, a flick of the wrist. "A horse can grow more hair on his ass. Esther needs it more on her head."

The horse hair was black and rich and heavy. They brushed it straight and sewed the ends of each hank into a cotton cap, then wound it around and around, shaping it into the upsweep and in-curl of the Gibson Girl hairdo. A little rouge for the cheeks, a little color on the lips . . . and *oy vey iz mir*, when she smiles it's like a cave with three bats in it hanging upside down. Where on the earth does a person get a mouth full of teeth?

"At the dentist of course. In this country they have everything, and you can buy it for money. But money we don't have—not for a full set of teeth, up and down. So I went to see Moishe Cohen the dentist in his office. He was a little man, so clean and neat, with a little beard and thick spectacles like small whiskey-glasses. What can I say to this man? A string of clever words, this-and-that, and I make a fool of him? Impossible. Nothing will do but the simple truth. 'Look, here it is: this is Isaacson's daughter. I owe the man my life, I must help his Esther or be ashamed before God and man. And Cohen! Consider that we hold here in our hands the happiness of a human being, of two human beings—even more, because I have a family myself, and there is one woman too many in my apartment.'

"So he looks me up, this dentist, and he looks me down. 'I

# Richard Slotkin

knew Isaacson,' he says. 'He was a *mensch*—an *edele mensch*,' he said. And it means. . . ?"

"It means he had a noble nature," I told him, "like a prince."

"Ah," said Zeydeh, satisfied, savoring the word. "That's right. Like a prince."

Then he continued: "So Cohen says, 'Pay me what you can, when you have it,' and without another word he puts her in his chair, pulls out the three teeth; makes a mold, and from that a cast, and from that two weeks later a set of big white beautiful American teeth."

"Moishe Cohen," Bubby sighed, "he should rest in peace, that just died in the *Forverts*."

Zeydeh said *Amen.*

Then: "So we cleaned her up, and she put on her dress out of the magazine and the button shoes, and the Gibson wig on her head, rouge on her face and lips. Then she put in her mouth the American teeth, topside and bottom side, gave a little bite to set them . . . and there she was. An American girl.

"What else is there to say? Moskowitz took one look at her with his sheep's eyes and discovered America yet another time."

"You made him a picture," said Bubby, "and he married the picture."

Zeydeh sighed. "You think I made a fool of him, to get her off my hands." He shrugged. Maybe he had. On the other hand. . . .

"Look: the man was no fool. It's true I didn't tell him her head was a room with no furniture. Sometimes the less a person knows the better off he is. He could see the good soul she was: it was in her eyes. If she talked like a child in Yiddish, in English she was a genius next to him, and his sister who didn't even have *his* three words. If you said hello she'd just smile and shake her head up and down and say, 'Da, da, da,' as if we were a bunch of Russians! When Esther came into their home they had more English than they knew what to do with. It didn't matter she couldn't cook. The sister was glad to remain queen of her kitchen and leave the rest to Esther.

# Greenhorns

By the time Moskowitz learned enough English to understand how simple she was, he didn't care. By then he knew what she was in herself: a good soul, a sweet nature, a loving heart. She was Isaacson's daughter—that's the first and last of it. Thirty years they lived man and wife—three children they had, that went to school, got married. . . . You can't do that with a magic trick, like snapping coins out of thin air. Laughing and singing around the house like a pet bird, that was no trick, it was her nature from when she was little. And when she looked at him it was like a kid with a birthday cake—she loved him that way. That was something."

Bubby lifted an eyebrow. "Nothing is made from nothing," she said.

Zeydeh conceded that much. "But," he said, "sometimes the Milkman reaches over and pulls a boiled egg out of your ear."

# Children, Drunks
## and
# the United States of America

In the summer of 1944 I was stationed at an Air Corps base in West Texas, in an endless plain of mesquite. The field was built to train air-crew for the B-29 Superfort, the new bomber designed to re-place the B-17 Flying Fortress for long-range missions.

The Superforts were gorgeous: huge shining steel and plexi-glass Death Angels, their wide graceful wingspan muscled up with four big engines, able to fly twice as far and half again as fast as the B-17, bearing unbelievable bomb-loads, complete catastrophe delivered right on target.

But there was something wrong with them. Although the engi-neers swore that they'd done the math, somehow the engines didn't have enough power to reliably lift a loaded Superfort into the air. If it was peacetime they'd have experimented till they got the aerody-namics adjusted or the engines properly souped up, but now there was no time to be careful. In the Pacific sailors and infantry had been dying in thousands to capture islands from which bombers could fly, and Japan was still beyond the range of the B-17. We had to have the Superforts, couldn't stop the assembly lines till they were perfected.

So they built the planes and sent them down to our base in West Texas to try out ways of getting them airborne: monkey with the afterburners, put baffles on the propellers to increase airflow, stretch the runway, change the angle of attack, fly tree-tops for the first two hundred miles to build speed and then start your climb. Half the test planes crashed in the mesquite, but it was so flat out there the pilots usually walked away. Since these test flights were also their training missions, the survivors got their ticket stamped and were shipped out to the Pacific. The Air Corps figured they knew at least one trick *not* to try when they started their taxi down the runway at Chungking or Saipan.

Meanwhile the engineers and photographers on our base would swarm out to photograph and diagram the ruins. We'd fire the pictures back to the factory, company engineers would adjust the machines while the assembly line was cranking along, and when the next batch dropped off the line they'd send some of *them* to West Texas so we could crash them into the mesquite.

It was the American way to fight a war: keep on building and smashing and building, throw everything into the fight, even the kitchen sink—especially the kitchen sink. We would expend vast energies, incalculable sums, oceans of blood and treasure, to save humanity from the murderous sneak-attacking Japanese and that maniac Hitler and his brood of cannibal supermen. Compared to our war aims, Woodrow Wilson's "Make the world safe for democracy" was the ambition of a beat cop. We were going to tear the world down and build it again in our own image—an American paradise, freedom and canned goods and cars for everybody from the little brown men in the jungle to the Frenchmen in Paris and the Swedes in Stockholm. Of course our means were extravagant, the overwhelming production and recruitment, scores of millions in uniform or at work in war plants; and the immense destructive firepower we brought to bear, reckless, the great cities of Europe and Japan lit off like firecrackers.

Later we remembered there were people in them. Extravagance is always careless: careless at heart about costs and consequences, which means it takes cruelty for granted. But of course we were spendthrift of our own lives as well. Perhaps that balances our account.

And the other side of extravagance is generosity—the uncalculated willingness of so many millions to serve. You felt you had to rise to such generosity in your own life. All the more so for me as a Jew. If I wasn't in America Hitler would have killed me already and everyone I loved along with me, and if America should be swept aside what could possibly save us? I don't know anyone who went through that time and did not feel in some way an immense obligation to do right by the nation—a feeling that (if you were eligible for combat) was coupled with the gut fear of personal death, which drove you in upon yourself in the most utterly selfish way imaginable. Draft-age men were asked to give all the blood of their bodies all the days and hours of the lives they would lose. I can't say I was eager to make that gift. But I did feel called upon. I *was* called. I went. I'd have gone as far as the service required. In the end, it did not ask me to give everything. I can't deny I'm grateful that it didn't.

I was drafted in 1942 and volunteered for the Air Corps. I had the idea that as a flier I would control my fate. The infantryman suffers all things, but the pilot of a plane (I thought) can fight or evade at will. This I surmised from my experience driving the delivery truck for my father's bakery. It was nonsense. The pilots who rode their Flying Forts into the German air over Europe flew in formations as rigid and hapless as those Light Brigade lancers who were shot to bits in an Errol Flynn picture I once saw.

I was lucky, losing those illusions didn't cost me my life. I washed out of pilot school because of a problem with my inner ear which spoiled my sense of balance at altitude. This problem had never arisen on the bakery truck. They transferred me to air-gunnery school. But the same problem that unfitted me to pilot the plane disabled me from defending it. I became the Air Corps' "white elephant," a possession of no apparent use which was somehow too valuable to throw away. They had me riding the rails from one end of the country to another as they absent-mindedly searched for some use they could put me to.

My wife Dolly wanted me to apply for a medical discharge. Dolly and I went back to second grade at PS 199—it seemed like we spent most of our childhood getting ready to marry each other. We finally made it after I graduated City College with a degree in accounting. When the war came we had been married two years; our first boy Sam was born three months after Pearl Harbor. We had just reached that stage when you feel that married is your *real* life, more completely your own than the twenty-odd years you were your parents' children. Then my notice came and *bang* it was over, I'm gone and she's thrown back into her parents' house, and except for this little stranger Sam what's left of our married life? Dolly's voice twisted and crackling on the long-distance line once a week . . . she was half my childhood and all my grown-up life and she was starting to fade out, becoming just a black-and-white photo, and if it ever got to where nothing was left but her picture then what would become of us?

But nobody got a medical out of Second Air Force. And the truth—which I didn't want to admit to my wife—the truth was, I didn't want to ask. My country had excused me from death and killing. It didn't seem right to beg off serving. There is a kind of moral economy in life, a balance between what you give and what you take. I was close enough to the edge as it was.

## 2

If it was up to my father, I would never have gone into the service at all. I'd have done what he did when the Czar's press gang came to get him for the Russo-Japanese War in 1904: throw some clothes in a bindle and smuggle myself across the border under a load of hay. In his case the border was Germany—in mine it would have been Mexico.

He was no soldier, but he had the courage of his convictions. Czar Nikolai was a half-imbecile blood-sucker whose idea of government was to turn the peasants and Cossacks and the ultra-nationalist Black Hundreds loose to murder the Jews whenever trouble threatened the regime. To kill or die for such a king and such a nation would have been (in my father's words) a shame and a corruption. Rather than be guilty of that he risked his life, and the lives of his wife and three sons, to blaze a trail for them to America. He saved my mother and my brother Sol, but the other two sons died before he could bring them out.

His body made the journey to America, but his head never quite caught up.

Inside our little bakery, my father was the master, completely at home. At the bread table he was an artist, mixing ingredients with precision, kneading with care, sure-handedly rolling out the loaves, especially his masterpiece, the big loaf we called "Korn bread": an over-size rye bread with a thick crisp crust and dense chewy body. Behind the counter he was the conductor of an orchestra, his music the play of words and sentiments between his customers and himself, in Yiddish and English and hybrids of the two, exchanging the little decencies that compose a neighborhood retail business— remembering the customer's preferences, asking after her children and grandchildren, showing concern for her family's health. When "Tante Mirel," the neighborhood crazy lady, wandered in with her hair and eyes wild with inexpressible terror, he would speak sooth- ingly and offer her a roll with butter—for madness there was no cure, but "at least you should take a bite to eat."

Outside that little world he was a harried exile, never sure of his welcome, never at ease in this country. He used to call police- men "Cossacks," and offer unasked-for bribes so they'd "let him keep the shop open." He kept expecting a visit from the American Black Hundreds, never seen but surely lurking somewhere in dark neighborhoods and the far suburbs where Jews were banned by covenant. You could explain a million times, he wouldn't believe the rules here were any different from Czarist Russia.

I was his "American" son, an unexpected and even embarrass- ing gift delivered when he and my mom had been years in this country and were in their forties—as puzzling to him as America itself.

My brother Sol, thirteen years older, raised me while Pop and

# Greenhorns

Mom were at the bakery. Sol put himself through City College to qualify as a CPA, and he saw to it that I followed in his footsteps—in the meantime teaching me enough book-keeping so I could do the accounts for our bakery. He also tried to interpret between me and the old man. He had his work cut out for him.

Starting from the time I took the civics course in high school, I made it my project to educate my father in the American way of life. This isn't the Old Country, I told him, there are opportunities here, for a Jew as much as for anyone else. Look at baseball, Pop: in this country a poor boy with nothing but his skills can earn a good living—get rich, even!—just playing ball. That was my own childhood American dream, but a poor choice for argument with my father. "Feh!" was his response. That a son should waste his time throwing a ball and hitting it with a stick was, to him, a shame and a corruption.

By the time I got to college it was clear that I would not be playing shortstop for the Dodgers. My lectures shifted from baseball to politics. In America you don't have to grub and pinch pennies to get by and keep one eye peeled for Cossacks. You have to "prime the pump" like Roosevelt says. Take a risk! Sure, it's hard times. But this is a rich country. So rich they don't call poor people poor, they call them "under-privileged."

But Pop had no more patience with my politics than he had with my baseball—the afternoons at Ebbets Field, the evenings at political rallies. The one was a shameful waste of time, but the other was worse: "Feh!" again, but now with panic in it, his brows clenched and the whites of his eyes showing. Politics was poison, it was dynamite, picking the wrong side could get us all dispossessed, thrown out of the country or killed.

Of course *he* voted for Roosevelt too, but that was different. Roosevelt was the President, the man in charge, it was safe to endorse him and dangerous not to. By that same logic he had voted for Harding and Coolidge and Hoover when *they* were in charge. But Pop went to the polls like a fugitive with warrants out for him.

99

# Richard Slotkin

A Jew could survive only by living like a turtle, pulling back into his shell at the first sign that *anything* might happen—good or bad made no difference, the safest thing was to pull everything inside and not stick your nose out till whatever was out there had gone away.

Mom would stay out of these arguments. She never said much at any time, maybe because she didn't have much English. Or maybe she thought talking was a waste of time. If Pop yelled at her in the store, or complained, or tried to argue with her, she'd shrug and go about her business. When Pop and I were going at it she'd stay close, as if maybe she'd have to jump in and save one of us. But if I gave her a look all she would say is, "Don't expect, you won't disappoint."

Her philosophy applied equally to my feelings about America and my arguments with Pop. But I couldn't let either one alone. I took Pop's fear as an insult, as if he was denying me my right to a good American life. Sure there are Jew-haters here like anywhere else, but they don't stop you earning a living or living a life. But Pop wouldn't see it. If Jews got by in America it was just luck—and luck can turn bad like *that*.

"A hundred sixty years there's been America, and you think it's *luck*?"

Pop would rear back, startled—that a son should talk back to a father? *That's* your America!

My brother Sol, to make peace, would joke: "The kid's right, Pop. God looks out for children, drunks, and the United States of America."

Pop didn't believe him, but he'd let the joke end the argument, shrug, wave his cigarette and blow us away like smoke, we were not people serious enough to argue with.

When I told him I got my draft notice he went white as death. "You ain't going," he said.

For a wild second I believed he had the power to forbid me to go in the army the way he used to forbid me to play baseball, and I thought *I'm saved*—then remembered that I never obeyed him about baseball, and this was more serious. To refuse the call was not only a criminal offense but, in the eyes of Jews and goyim alike, a shame and a corruption.

But to Pop conscription was a death-sentence. A Jew drafted into the Czar's army was taken for fifteen or twenty years, and if the denial of his religion did not destroy his soul, with the mistreatment he'd suffer from those Jew-hating Russian bastards he'd die till he got out. No use to tell Pop the American army was different. An army is an army. "They want to kill him, that's all!" he cried. He wasn't even talking to me but to Sol—I was beyond reasoning with, always had been, the "American" son. There was no pacifying him, either. As soon as Sol opened his mouth Pop shut it for him: "And don't make a goddamn joke of it, with your drunks and your children!" He was shaking with anger and fear for me. But that just scared me more, and I was already terrified enough, so I let myself get mad and storm out of the house.

I'm sorry now that I didn't show more respect for his opinion. What he knew he knew from life and not from books. And he wasn't wrong about armies. Russian or American they do, mostly, try to kill you. I was lucky. Pop just couldn't believe that his child might have that kind of luck, or divine protection, like drunks and the United States of America.

He died right after I washed out of pilot training. My first furlough was granted to attend his funeral—which was also the last time I would see Dolly for more than a year.

## 3

The Air Corps paid my expenses for a grand tour of the country, bouncing me from one posting to another in search of a use for my skills.

I had grown up in Brownsville Brooklyn dreaming of America: gazing down the harbor at the Great Green Lady, still holding aloft the lamp that welcomed my parents and my friends' parents and grandparents to America, to the blessed and beautiful country, the spacious skies, the amber waves, the brotherhood from sea to sea. The truth is that ninety percent of what goes on in this country happens behind the Lady's back. The amber waves are there, the spacious skies. Brotherhood I found in short supply.

The real revelation of that journey was that, despite being a natural-born American, I was still essentially a greenhorn, thunderstruck by the strangeness of the people among whom I now found myself—puzzled to know how or if I fit in. Where I came from in Brooklyn, people showed their love of country by hanging the portrait of Abraham Lincoln on the kitchen wall right next to the one of Karl Marx—a state of mind incomprehensible to the boys from Toledo and Omaha and Pascagoula with whom I was thrown together. Out here I was an alien, and they let me know it. Now and then I'd hear the word *kike*, and once a bunk-mate asked in all innocence to feel my head to see if I had horns. But that kind of thing was rare enough. Mostly it was the way some non-coms, if I pissed them off, would tack a "You people" on to whatever they were bawling me out for, as in "Why is it You People can't shoot a fucking rifle?" As if my failures proved the uselessness of my race. In a way the worst were the throw-away insults, "Son of a bitch tried to jew me down"—as if me and mine were mere figures of speech, not actual persons who had ears to hear and feelings to be outraged.

"Don't expect, you won't disappoint," my mother would have said. But I did expect, I was disappoint. My antidote to that estrangement was to grab my old baseball mitt and a rubber ball out of my footlocker, find myself an empty space behind a warehouse or motor pool garage, bang the ball against the wall and dream I was back home in Brooklyn and the Dodgers were playing. I'd bounce a grounder off the wall, scoop it like Reese at shortstop and peg it to Camilli at first. I'd replay all the Dodger games I could remember, inning by inning, the way they really happened and the way they *could* have. Suppose Mickey Owen doesn't drop that third strike in the '41 Series. Do we win the game, pull even with the Yanks and win the Series in seven?

But after a while my game went sour. Living in a dream of Brooklyn instead of dealing with the country around me was no better than Pop refusing to see Brooklyn as anything different from the *shtetl* he escaped. At my next-to-last posting I haunted the base sergeant-major, pestered him to search his listings for a permanent assignment, ignoring his habit of referring to "You People" every time I asked. And one fine day a request came through for a photographer at that West Texas air base. "Can you take pitchers?" he asked. "Like Cecil B. DeMille," I told him. "Fuck you and Cecil both," he said, and stamped my papers for me.

Which was how I found myself out in God's country, taking pictures of smashed Superforts.

# 4

The sun slammed down on that plain like a hammer on an anvil and shook the dust loose. Dust got into everything, shoes, food, teeth. The air was so dry it cracked the planks of the barracks walls and the dust drifted inside.

But at least I had something to do which the Army thought useful. And I was in cowboy country, Western movie country—every Brooklyn boy's image of the real, the pure America. The Rio Grande ran a few miles west of the base, the border whose defense had been the business of cowboys and cavalry—the border I would have fled across if I had imitated my father. That I would never do. America was my country. I belonged to it and it to me. If I ever had to leave it, I would be an exile all my days. But what I knew of it from my Brooklyn childhood was mostly dreams, and what I had learned of it in my travels was a puzzle. Maybe I could see my country clearer if I stepped over the border-line and looked at it from outside.

So when I finally got a three-day pass I decided to catch the overnight bus to El Paso, some 500 miles away across the desert.

# Richard Slotkin

The trip would take about fifteen hours. There was an exhibition of photographs at the Art Museum that I wanted to see—I was beginning to think of myself as a professional photographer. Then I'd cross the border to Juarez and buy some gifts for my mom and Dolly, and Dolly's mom and Sol's wife. Spend the night in El Paso and catch the noon bus back.

The bus was a rusty old wheezer, its sides sandblasted down past the primer by the all-fired West Texas dust. I climbed aboard and sidled up the aisle. It was a small bus, with seats for only thirty passengers, six of them in the Colored section at the rear. All the seats were taken except for one near a window in the Colored section, but that seat was busted. There was an old Colored man in the aisle seat next to it. He paid me no mind. I dropped my overnight bag in the aisle and took hold of the bar, figuring to stand till someone got off.

The bus never moved. The driver raised his head to the round mirror that looked down the aisle of the bus. "Boy," he said, "That sojer's waitin' on you."

The people on the bus stilled. The old man went stiff as a stick. There were four Colored women in the back too: I saw them drop their heads to stare into their laps. The old man's white hair showed plain against his dark skin. I was embarrassed a man the same age as my Pop should be called *Boy* and told like a child to get up and give me his seat.

"That's okay," I said, "I don't mind."

There was dead silence in the bus. It was as if I hadn't said anything at all. As if there was nothing there of me but my uniform and my white face.

The driver called out, "Boy I'm waitin' on you."

The silence on the bus was alive with expectation. Everything about this moment was shameful, but I couldn't think how to change it. Would it do any good to *shout* what I'd said? To make a scene? But how would it end?

The old man heaved himself up. "Dat's all right," he said softly,

104

# Greenhorns

"give my seat to one our boys in suyvice." The four Colored women murmured fierce approval, as if the old man's courtesy had bettered the driver's insult. Two of them squeezed together to let the old man perch on the end of their seat.

The driver racked the bus into gear and we started for El Paso. The people in the White section began to jabber together again, someone guffawed and a woman said, "Oh you Jasper!" like she was proud of a naughty thing her man had said.

The shame of it was on me, not just the old man. It wasn't just helpless I'd felt, it was *afraid*—afraid to go up against the people on the bus, who were sure that the black man would have to knuckle under, and anticipated the pleasure they'd feel when their expectations were met. Pop might be wrong in thinking there were Black Hundreds in Brooklyn waiting their chance to come knocking at his door. But where Colored people were concerned, plenty of Americans shared a Black-Hundreds state of mind.

Yet what could I have done? Made them a speech how much better life would be if we just showed each other a little neighborly respect? Asked after the family, offered someone a buttered roll? I suppose that out of two dozen white people on that bus there might have been one or two who would have responded to an appeal to simple decency. Even in Texas. But I'd missed that chance.

Then it hit me that I'd just been freely given something I and all my friends and family always doubted we'd get: simple and unquestioning recognition as "an American like everybody else." Which is to say, like every-*white*-body else. With admission to that club came the privilege of joining in the national pastime of hazing Colored people. Or if not *joining in*, at least *consenting to*—because here I was sitting in the old man's seat.

When I looked back to see how he was doing he was staring straight ahead, hard-eyed and rigid, and would not let his eyes touch me. For as long as we rode the bus neither he nor the Colored women gave any indication they knew I existed. I had the freedom of the country. Their approval was not included in the deal.

## 5

Three in the morning the bus stopped for gas and the driver couldn't start it again. We were at a little gas station and eatery out in the chaparral. Talk about "dark fields of the republic," you haven't seen *dark* till you've been out in the West Texas desert at three in the morning. The sky overhead was huge, lit up with a million stars like New York City at Christmas. But the terrain below was a flat dead black that ate the starlight and sucked up the lightspill from the gas station after a dozen yards.

If I had to wait for the next bus I'd have no time in El Paso before I had to turn around and go back. But if a car or truck came along I could almost surely hitch a ride. Everybody stopped to give soldiers a lift in those days. You didn't worry they might be criminals—it was a different time, more generous or maybe just more careless.

I sat on my overnight bag at the roadside for about a half hour. Then down at the end of the long straight run of highway I saw a couple of headlights coming on fast and a few minutes later a big Dodge sedan fishtailed in off the road, spun its wheels in the dirt and screeched to a stop at an eccentric angle to the gas pumps. My luck was in.

I got to the door in time to help the driver out. He needed all the help he could get. The smell of gin that came off him was enough to gag a Bowery bum. He grinned lopsided at me, his blue eyes swimming. He was maybe forty, pink-skinned and fair-haired, and he wore a nicely made white suit and blue bow-tie. The hand he gave me to haul him out of the seat had a big gold ring on it. I said, "Say, if you'll give me a ride to El Paso, I'll fill her up while you. . . ."

He beamed at me: "Use the can! Sure, you bet—take all soldiers I can fit. Got one in back already. Tell you what though—can you drive? Because this ration-book gin we're drinking is wearing me out."

He'd been drinking steadily since Dallas, which he'd left some unremembered time and six hundred miles ago. How he made it that far alive I couldn't tell you. "Children, drunks, and the United States of America." I never figured out why he was drinking so hard. Maybe my mistake, easy to make when you're from *shtetele* Brooklyn, was thinking there had to be a reason. The way he spoke about it, loading up on gin for a long drive was like filling the tank with gas, machine don't run without it. It was just what a man did, like wearing the best clothes you could buy if you had money— which he had. Gas and tires were rationed. You didn't take off a thousand miles into the desert unless you weren't worried about the coupons. So he was making money out of the war, which even if you were legal had to make you feel a little crooked. Maybe that was why the gin. Maybe I'm making it up.

Anyway, he needed me to drive because he couldn't go on drinking and driving, and the drinking was more important. So we shook on it. I pumped the car full. He took a leak, then came back and opened the passenger-side door. He looked thoughtful. There was a woman in the front seat, passed out, "My wife." Her head was thrown back like her neck had a hinge in it, snoring open-mouthed. "Let's move her in back."

But there was somebody in back already—the soldier the man said he'd picked up, a Marine buck sergeant in a green uniform that had been slept and puked in. His chest was full of ribbons. He was passed-out drunk too. His head was wrapped in a bandage that covered his right eye. I lifted his legs and eased them over.

Meanwhile the man had got his wife's legs into his arms, but tipped her over so she sprawled into the driver's seat. She was slim and had a narrow pale face and very thin lips, very delicate looking, but the gin put her so far out there was no *lift* to her, she was made entirely of bone. We wrestled her into the back seat and sat her up, knocking knees with the Marine but leaning against the opposite side of the car. Then the man—Yarbrough was his name— Yarbrough grinned, pulled another bottle out of the trunk of the car, and got in next to me.

As we pulled out he asked, "Know who that is in back?" I didn't. "Kid Kelleher! Used to pitch for the Yankees."

*Shit*, I thought, *Kid Kelleher!* "Not the Yankees," I told him, "It was Brooklyn he pitched for."

Yarbrough didn't buy it: "*Dem* Bums?" The universal moniker of the Dodgers expressed his scorn. "Listen, this guy's a hero. Got the Silver Star or something. You say he played for *Brooklyn*?"

Yarbrough was proud of having Kid Kelleher in his back seat, never mind him playing for Brooklyn. A major league pitching star. A war hero. He'd picked him up just outside of Dallas, walking straight west along the highway like he was on a mission. Yarbrough pulled over to offer him a lift—a soldier, convalescent, it was what you did. Wife had to holler and whistle to get his attention. "He had a good load on already," Yarbrough said. "`Where you goin'?' I ask him. `Where *you* goin'?' he says. 'El Paso.' 'Well that's where I'm goin'.'" So they celebrated their meeting with the gin, Kelleher flopped in the back seat, and Yarbrough "pointed them West." The Kid drank quiet. But what with winking and smiling, the wife got him to say who he was and they drank to baseball and the Yankees. Kelleher must have been plastered past caring if he drank *that* toast.

Yarbrough went on: "I asked him, 'You on a pass?' He just says, 'Fuck it.'" Yarbrough shook his head. "Didn't bother him the wife was sitting there." He shrugged it off: kind of thing you let go if it was a soldier, especially wounded.

## 6

I drove pretty fast, no other cars, just the slot of highway cut through the sagebrush. Yarbrough dozed off. I tilted the mirror so I could see Kelleher in the back seat. There was a bulge under the bandage where his right eye should be.

Kid Kelleher was a Brooklyn boy who made it through the farms and up to the big club right before the war. He was a *phen*om, wild but fast. The papers used to say how if he ever learned to control that speed it's the second coming of Walter Johnson. I saw him pitch at Ebbets Field a few times: a thrower, but he could *throw*. It was like watching some terrible machine to see him tear through a lineup throwing nothing but fastballs. Then along about the sixth inning he'd lose control and there wasn't any place in the park that was safe. He had all the gifts, though. A little seasoning and he's the stopper the Dodgers never had since Dazzy Vance. When he left the park after a game, kids waited by the players' exit and walked off after him like a parade. He had a big contract too, big for a rookie in those days, and drove a red convertible.

He had all the gifts, and he knew it. Thought like a hero, carried himself that way, expected big things to be expected of him, he could handle it all. The war came and he enlisted in the Marines. It was what Kid Kelleher would do. They made a parade of him there too: did a training film in which he shows you how to pitch a grenade. But the story was he wanted combat (it was what Kid Kelleher *would* want), and the Marines obliged. He was on Guadalcanal, saw a lot of action. Knocked out a machine gun pitching grenades (or that was the story) and won a medal. Then he was wounded by shrapnel from a mortar shell and shipped back to the States. He was supposed to do a War Bond drive with other decorated Marines, but it never happened, they said on account of complications with the wound. Still, the papers said his pitching arm was okay. Great sighs of relief in Brooklyn.

Now it turned out it wasn't his arm, it was his eyes. Or one of them, as it seemed by the look of him in the rear-view mirror, sprawled drunk in the back of the Dodge. His bandage burned blue in the night light. His head was lolling a little, side to side. Then he slumped so his head dropped onto young Missus Yarbrough's shoulder. It might have been that he just slid that way, asleep or drunk; but then he shifted his butt to get right next to her, his face buried in her neck, and he reached up and filled his hand with her right breast. She was still out cold, head back like her neck was broken. The road ahead ran straight as a ruled line into the dead black beyond the reach of the headlamps. When I glanced back in the mirror the Kid was kneading her breast with his fingers and hand. It seemed to almost get through to her, she kept trying to raise her head up out of the gin, brushing vaguely at his hand till she knocked it off her breast down onto her lap.

I couldn't see what happened down there but *something* did, for it woke her up. Her head still wobbled like it was on loose, but she wriggled and worked him off with her hands and arms. Yarbrough was still snoring away. Generosity to soldiers was the rule, but Kelleher was pushing it. When I glanced back in the mirror again they had quieted down, the Kid had his head wedged in the groove between her shoulder and her breast and she was letting him keep it there. She was willing to do him that much kindness, though not as much as he wanted—and they were both passed out again.

When we pulled over so Yarbrough could take a piss, Kelleher woke up too, staggered out and stood half-bent, one hand leaning on the fender, while he peed on Yarbrough's black market tires. Yarbrough handed him the gin bottle and he glugged it. Missus Y was still asleep. I said why didn't Yarbrough sit in back with his wife? Kelleher didn't realize what had happened till he opened the back door and saw Yarbrough in his seat. He muttered something, slammed the door, and came around to sit next to me in the front.

He sat a while staring out at the headlights swallowing the endless line of road. He said, "Okay then *fuck* it." Not yelling, just saying it. Then he slammed his fist hard into the padded door-panel. "I'm *fucked* I stand for this." *Slam.*

He was drunk out of his mind, a twenty-two year-old kid angry and probably going nuts on account of his eye. Okay. But also a *big* kid, strong, and dangerous if he started punching me while we were speeding down the highway. *Change the subject. Cheer him up.* "I'm from Brooklyn myself," I told him. "I saw you pitch—the time you two-hitted Cincinnati?"

"The fuck is that to me?" he barked, "I'm done with it!"

*Done with it.* So the eye was gone? I wanted to ask him, but he was glaring at me like he was looking for an excuse to slug me.

Yarbrough suddenly stuck his face between us, leaning over the seat-back. "Son," he said, "what you need is some pussy to set you to rights." His voice dropped to a discreet whisper, bearing in mind the Missus snoring behind him. "When we get to Paso what you do is, you go over the bridge to Juarez City. Ask for Cortez Street, it runs along the river. Man it's a whole neighborhood of nothin' but *putas*. Walkin' nekkid in the streets! Say what? I'll give you some *money*! Hell, it ain't any more'n you got coming, what *you* done."

Kelleher reared around, blinking one-eyed for a look at the man, "Fuck *you* say I got coming!" he was looking for a fight, a fight was what he wanted right *now*.

"Here y'are Kid," said Yarbrough, leaning over to jam a wad of bills in his breast pocket. "Take that to Cortez Street and get yourself *properly* fucked. By God, you earned yourself a piece of the best there is."

Even Kelleher couldn't make a fight out of that. The best he could manage was to take the gift as no more than he deserved. "Goddamn right," he said, and went to sleep on it.

## 7

Kelleher and I got out at the USO, which was located in the downtown YMCA. I thanked Yarbrough for the lift, but he waved it off: neither one of us would have gotten out of the desert if it wasn't for the other. We were even. Yarbrough told Kelleher good-bye good-luck. The Kid didn't thank him for the ride or the money, let alone the feel of his wife. Took it as his due. As the car pulled away he just stood in the street, rocking a little like in a wind although there wasn't a moving breath in that street, hot as an oven and it wasn't nine o'clock. He turned his head till he found the sun and had to wring his one eye shut. Then he started walking in that direction, east.

# Richard Slotkin

"Hey," I said, "where are you going?"

He took two steps and stopped and stood swaying. Then he said, "Juarez," like it's any of my business.

"Wrong way," I said and when he turned I pointed south to the international bridge. He didn't thank me either, just came stalking back past me. "You ought to go in the Y and clean up," I told him. He was puked and unshaved and dirty, even a blind MP would arrest him by the smell. "Fuck if it don't suit *you*," he said and kept on walking, down Texas Street and around the corner. They'd never let him through the border post. But it was probably better he got arrested before he did anything crazy.

I took my own advice, washed up and left my bag at the Y, had breakfast, went to the Museum. But I couldn't seem to pay attention to the photos. I kept thinking about Kelleher. So since I planned to go over to Juarez anyway, I walked down to the Rio Grande bridge a little after noon. The American border guards checked my papers and my pass and told me I had to be back on our side by sunset. I asked the corporal if he'd seen a Marine with a bandaged head and he grinned, "Sure. Kid Kelleher! He crossed over this morning." I guess if you are Kid Kelleher they do what you want, never mind what you look or smell like.

"You a buddy of his?" the MP corporal asked skeptically. If I was, maybe he'd have to do *me* a favor.

"No—just an acquaintance."

"Didn't think so," he said disdainfully and waved me on.

I was a little concerned about The Kid. Maybe the MPs would give him a pass for being out of bounds, but Mexico was another story. If he remembered Yarborough's advice he'd be down on Cortez Street, so I thought I'd go there first.

I crossed the Rio Grande into Mexico. The idea of it hit me when I was half way over—the Rio Grande, Gary Cooper or Buck Jones would pause and take a good long look before they crossed it, the great border river of the west.

This was what Pop did when he was young: crossed the border

112

to another country. But he was running from the army of a nation he hated and that hated him, and once across he was never going back. For me it was different. The Mexican border cops passed me through dead-pan, just another gringo. I never felt more American in my life than right then.

Knowing I had America behind me, I looked at Juarez like a man with a license to cut loose. Take what you like and enjoy yourself, nothing here is your problem. I wondered if Pop ever felt that free, when he got off the boat in New York, alone and a stranger, wife and children ten thousand miles away, the whole city waiting and nobody to answer to but himself. He'd been away from Mom, presumably celibate, for more than a year. There must have been a counterpart to Cortez Street on the Lower East Side. If I had to guess I'd say he probably pulled into his shell so he wouldn't see anything but what was right in front of him and started pushing blindly ahead—but maybe not. After all, he'd had the gall to pull himself up by the roots and get out of Russia. It was a subject that, until that moment, it had never even occurred to me to ask about— not that I ever could have. Already Mexico was giving me a new angle on my life in the States.

I myself wasn't brash enough to ask directions to Cortez Street. What would these people think of me if I asked them the way to the whores? Anyway, Yarbrough said it ran along the river, so I poked around in that direction.

Turned a corner and suddenly I was there—knew it because it was just the way Yarbrough described it.

Understand that it was hot down there, the kind of heat that made you want to take your skin off. There was a little plaza, sun-blasted yellow stone and bright green yuccas like shell-bursts and these spindly palm trees with dark dusty-green leaves, and lolling around in the shade were more than a dozen women, most of them mostly naked, just these transparent gauze shifts. Like a Gauguin painting, women and young girls with black eyes, bronzy gold skin and lush falls of black hair, brown nipples and a little black tuft right *there*, only they were smoking these sloppy cigarettes. They didn't seem to care if you looked, they were what they were, no shame in it. It was another country *entirely*. "Hola gringo!" they called, and a sweet young thing who really knew how to flatter a buck private even called me "Senor Sergente!"

Well I wanted to—who wouldn't? Paradise! The American dream, to cross the border and find paradise and indulge yourself— extravagantly! I wondered if Kid Kelleher was inside already, the hero enjoying himself on a heroic scale.

I felt something peculiar, as if I somehow peeled away from myself, and part of me is thinking *all I have to do is pay the man with the mustache and it's mine, paradise!*—and the other part is saying *this can't be happening to the Jewish kid from Brooklyn, Mom and Pop's boy, Sol's kid brother, Dolly's husband Sam's father*, but they were so small and far away, just black and white photos. . . .

*And if you do it*, I said inside, *you won't ever be the man that can go back to them.*

Pop's turtle wisdom coming to his son's rescue, I suppose. I backed out of there, smiling like an idiot so they wouldn't take offense. It's not for me. It's not for *me*. I don't judge, but it's not for me.

I felt a little deflated. As if I had backed down from a challenge.

I found my way to the main plaza, where the silver sellers kept their booths in a long relatively cool arcade off the main plaza. I shopped my way down the rows, one hand brushing my wallet, afraid of pickpockets. One old fellow caught my eye. He had some trays of bracelets and earrings, some beaten-metal and some in that real Mexican silver lacework I was looking for. There was something about the guy I liked. He smiled and nodded a little, as if all he meant was a friendly greeting, pass on or stay, as you like, you were welcome all the same. His eyes had a melancholy droop at the corners and his left eyebrow was cocked up in a way that suggested a sort of genial skepticism.

# Greenhorns

So I said "Buenos dias" and he said "Good afternoon. I am called Nacio Alvarez." I told him my name and we shook hands. Then he settled in his chair and watched patiently while I looked over his goods.

Right away I saw the lacework bracelet I wanted for Dolly, and a ring her mom would like; a nice pair of earrings that was also modest enough that my mom might actually wear them, and another pair just right for Sol's wife. But by the tags they cost way too much.

"What do you like?" said the old man.

"The problem is, I don't have the money for what I like."

He waved that away. That was not what he asked. We were not haggling, we were two men discussing the beauty of certain objects.

Well, I admitted, there was this bracelet, very beautiful, for my wife but. . . .

He fended off my objections with the palms of his hands, shut his eyes against them. "You like it," he said. "We put it *aside*." And he laid it on a piece of velvet-covered board. "What else do you like?"

Well, as one man to another, these earrings were very nice. "For my mother."

Your mother? Good. He was pleased. We understood one another. "We put them aside."

And then the ring, "For my wife's mother."

He nodded a deeper approval, his eyes half-closed. I was a serious person, one who gave consideration to the mother of his wife. And was there more I liked?

These earrings. "For my brother's wife."

Ah. "You are a man rich in family," he said, leaving unsaid *though poor in dollars*. The earrings too we put aside. "And this is all?"

"Yes," I said, "but I haven't got enough money to buy them all at that price." The tags added up to forty dollars.

This too he did not wish to hear. I had misunderstood him. "What do you have to pay for them?"

I needed a few bucks for supper and bus fare back to the base. Beyond that I had twenty dollars. I looked at the man and he looked right back, and I knew if I said I had fifteen dollars he'd probably take it. And he'd probably know I was holding out on him too. He'd think badly of me. It would spoil the conversation we'd just been having, one man to another.

So I told him, "I've got twenty to spend."

"Let it be twenty then," he said, and when I thanked him he flicked it away with his fingers. One man does not thank another for dealing justly with him. He wrapped each item in tissue paper and put the balls of paper in a little cloth sack. I gave him the money and we shook hands and wished each other well.

That exchange left me feeling happy, in a way I hadn't felt for a long time. *Satisfied* I guess, that's what I felt. And soothed, after all the stress and worry and fear I'd been living through. Making all due allowance for the difference of local manners, Nacio Alvarez sold silver the same way that Pop sold bread: with care for the goods and for the customer's feelings, for the small decencies of a neighborhood retail business. There was nothing extra about it, nothing too much or too little. There was balance. Give and take. Nobody got charity, but nobody got screwed either. From each, considering his resources, to each according to his wish, and vice versa. Not exactly Karl Marx, but close enough. And the little sack of paper-wrapped silver was like a talisman to bring me safe home.

## 8

The late afternoon sun was slanting down and I walked back toward the Rio Grande bridge through sharp wedges of shadow. A couple of blocks from the border I saw Kelleher hanging onto a light-post with one hand and barking out short angry bursts of English at the Mexicans walking past him—who swerved to pass the drunk dirty gringo at a safe distance.

# Greenhorns

He didn't know where he was or how to get where he wanted to go. The way he moved his head around made me think even his good eye must not be so good. I felt bad, suddenly, for how I'd let him wander off alone, how I'd left off looking for him after stumbling into that paradise on Cortez Street.

I said "Hey Kid," and he swung around to point his face at me. "Who the fuck are you?" he wanted to know, so I told him but couldn't tell if he remembered the guy who drove him across the desert. "I was just going back over to Paso," I told him. "Let's us both go back."

"Fuck Paso," he said, "all I want is for you to point me at those whores you were talkin' about." So he remembered the car, but couldn't tell me from Yarbrough.

"It's getting late," I told him. "Our passes are no good after dark. Mexican cops will throw us in one of their jails all night, then turn us over to the MPs."

He poked his face at me, and banged me in the chest with two pointed fingers: "Where are those whores you were talkin' about, or was it all bullshit?" Then he threw a contemptuous wave at the whole street and blared his complaint as loud as he could, "*These* fuckin' people don't know *shit!*"

Most of those fuckin' people were paying us no mind, as if it was not polite to acknowledge the follies of drunkards. But there were three or four men watching us from the shadow of a cantina doorway who were taking notice. Maybe they even understood English.

I took hold of his arm. "I take you anywhere but back, you will get yourself beat up or killed."

He gave me a look that said I was a moron. "The fuck I care," he said. "Kill me okay, but fuck if I'll sit on my ass the rest of my life and watch myself die. Fuck if I will."

That was the word of Kid Kelleher, the Brooklyn *phe*nom. He was going blind, he was losing everything he had or could have imagined for himself—and my god, what he would have imagined

117

# Richard Slotkin

for himself would have been tremendous, glorious, heroic. You'd have to be Kid Kelleher to know what else there was in his life that could sustain him. But he *was* Kid Kelleher and he couldn't think of anything but blowing his wad in a Mexican whore house.

For everything he was and everything he stood for and everything he'd done, I owed it to him to help. But how? I could leave him there, where he was likely to get into a street fight with the cantina boys, and get himself knifed or thrown in jail or both. Or I could direct him to the whores on Cortez Street, where he could take his pleasure—though given his mood and his drunkenness his pleasure too might involve picking a fight. I was stuck with a set of choices none of which would do the least bit of good for me or the person I wanted to help—the same as it was with the old black man on the bus. But then I had passed up the chance to make a little speech about the small decencies that make a good life. Maybe it would work now.

So I gave it a try. I tried to imagine what Mom and Pop would have said to their American son if I had suffered a disaster like the one that hit Kelleher. It occurred to me that they'd have been better prepared for such a misfortune than for the good luck and brilliant promise of my American dream. Pop might have been wrong to worry about Cossacks, but he was right about the main thing: even in America, it was possible for things to go terribly, irredeemably wrong. He had come through such disasters himself, and not been broken by them. He'd have told me to pass through the pain, get over the *kholeria*, bury your dead and mourn for them—then gather what resources were left and take up again the business of living, with the same patient care he gave to composing his loaves of bread, and to the retail decencies of neighborhood life.

So I offered that to Kelleher. You've lost plenty, I told him, no question about that. But you're still alive, you're young, you can live a good life—like everyone else!—a useful trade, maybe coaching, a wife and kids. And better than that: "You're luckier than most, you're a man people respect—a man people will care about."

# Greenhorns

He just kept staring steadily at me, his lips pinched together, waiting for me to stop blethering and tell him the way to Cortez Street. I remembered Pop trying to ease Tante Mirel's lunacy with a roll and butter, or telling me to count my blessings twice and don't let the Cossacks see where I stash them, and Mom warning, "Don't expect, you won't disappoint." I didn't listen to them and Kelleher wasn't listening to me. Still, my good intentions may have gotten through to him, because he didn't tell me to shut the fuck up. Just stood there and listened till I was done. Then he said, "You know where those whores are or don't you?"

There was no talking to him. He was hell bent on what he wanted. Probably being hell-bent was what had made him what he was as a pitcher and as a soldier. It was who he was. What was I supposed to do about it?

What popped into my head was my brother Sol's joke about God watching out for children, drunks, and the United States of America. In this case I was God's stand-in, and for the first time I sympathized with His problem. Kelleher was an overgrown child, a drunk, and a true American hero. Born lucky, favored by God and nature with such an abundance of gifts, so full of potential, and weirdly innocent—not devoid of meanness or cruelty, just blind to the costs he imposed on others by having things his own way. But when the luck fails, and the gifts are wasted or used up, does God say, "All right! Enough is enough! Now sober up, pay your fine, and learn to settle for just being a decent little person, a decent little nation, living a decent little life."

I don't know about God, but I didn't have the heart to say it. So I told him how to get to Cortez Street. Maybe it *was* doing him a kindness. Yarbrough thought it was, that careless prodigal drunk. And it was what he wanted. If it wasn't what he ought to want, was it my job to put him straight?

"Is it as good as you said?"

I'm thinking, wait till he gets a load of that plaza, dozens of women naked in the heat lounging under the palm trees, all they ask is money and he's got plenty of that. "How good can you see?" I asked him.

"Good enough to get laid with."

"It's even better than I said."

He made a mouth at me, did I take him for a jerk? "Listen, bud: you want to do me a favor, just point me where they're at."

So I walked him part of the way down to Cortez Street. I hoped he could see well enough to appreciate that plaza full of naked brown women. He wouldn't back away from it the way I had. He'd think it was just what Kid Kelleher had coming. Paradise. Maybe it would satisfy him. I didn't think it would, not for long anyway. But don't expect and you won't disappoint.

When we got close enough to hear the chatter of the women in the plaza I said "So long. And watch the clock. You don't want to spend the night in a Mexican jail." He just waved and kept walking.

I told myself I had done what I could for him, but I still hung around for an hour, listening to hear if he had started a brawl down the street, hoping he'd come out and I could see him safe back to the USA. But why would he leave paradise before he had to? I had to catch the bus tomorrow noon or go AWOL, and what good would that do him? So I went back across the bridge, ate supper, slept at the Y. I spent the next morning walking back and forth between the Y and the bridge, hoping Kelleher would show, but I never saw him again.

## 9

It stormed like hell on the ride back. I remember when I got to the base early next morning it was completely socked in with fog. Like you were half blind and had cotton stuffed in your ears. As I walked back to my quarters the broke-bodied ghost of a Superfort materialized in front of me, one of the smash-ups they'd hauled in off the desert to study for clues. The whole huge waste of it. I went right to the PX and mailed my gifts home. Then I put in a long distance call to Dolly, Sam was awake and he made a noise into the phone that sounded like pigeons.

# Greenhorns

Three months later, I read in the papers that Kelleher put a pistol in his mouth and killed himself.

## 10

Everything else turned out more or less okay. The Superforts got fixed and fire-bombed the Japanese cities for a whole year, and then they laid the two Big Ones on Hiroshima and Nagasaki. I remember how we all cheered, happy for the guys who wouldn't have to get killed trying to fight those mad-men on their own ground— and bowled over by the sheer power of it, just one bomb and *boom* there goes a whole city. Later on there was a horror to it, all those women and children incinerated in a flash, but even then you said *well better theirs than ours*. And besides, if we invaded we'd have had to kill them house by house, so if you think about it they're *lucky* it was just two cities . . . and God save *us* from such luck.

As for me, I got home eighteen months later, no harm done either way. My life was still there waiting for me, and I took it up again. I guess the only difference is, I was so grateful just to have it back. I'm careful of it now, as Pop was careful—though I don't worry as much as he did about Cossacks. Still sometimes I wake up at night, shaking, from dreams in which I am cut loose by some careless swipe or blow of fate from everything I love and everyone that loves me.

# Uncle Max and Cousin Yossi

There's an old vaudeville tune my dad used to sing me when I was little.

> Last night I saw upon the stair
> A *Little Man* who wasn't there.
> He wasn't there again today—
> O how I wish he'd go away!

A joke. How could someone *be* there who *wasn't* there? Then one night as I slid to sleep I *saw* him—a Little Man horribly watching us from the top of a high stair, just glimpsed before he flashed into never-being. I woke! It felt like an escape.

It turned out there *was* a Little Man, and he belonged to our family. He was called "Cousin Yossi," but his name was seldom spoken. As far as I know our family preserved only two images of him.

The first I saw when I was six, sitting with my Zeydeh and looking through the pictures in his old leather-bound album. On one page was a faded sepia-tone of a family group, the men in frock coats, the women in long dresses with ruffled fronts. It was taken in 1908, a few years after Zeydeh brought his older brother Isaac and his family from Russia to America. In the center were the two brothers: a fresh-faced and boldly mustachioed Zeydeh with an astonishing head of dark curly hair; and next to him Uncle Isaac, with a full rabbinical beard, embroidered skull cap, and eyebrows quizzically raised. Zeydeh moved his finger from face to face, naming Bubby (my grandmother who had died when I was an infant), and their children clustered around them: apple-cheeked Uncle Abe, the eldest, then sixteen years old, the only one of their surviving children born on the Other Side; Uncle Mel, who even then looked like he had been sucking lemons; and Aunt Rochelle, now a kindly fussy old yenta, then a princess doll with flowers in her hair. My father was not there—he would not be born until nine years later.

At Uncle Isaac's side was his wife, my Tante Sarah—both of them died long before I was born—and their son Max, who we called "Uncle Max" even though he was only a cousin. And in front of Max (who was then about thirteen years old) was a little boy with hair so blond it made a white blaze in the photograph. Zeydeh's finger hesitated, then touched the blaze. "Yossi," he said, "your cousin Yossi. Him you never met. He's not with us." That seemed to mean that Yossi, like Bubby and Uncle Isaac and Tante Sarah, was dead. But before I could ask he flipped the page and changed the subject, "Look! Your daddy here, when he is just a baby!"

The second photograph of Yossi I did not see until fifteen years later, in 1962. It was a snapshot taken in 1930, probably by Max since he wasn't in the frame. Zeydeh and Bubby were seated on a picnic bench, smiling stiffly for the camera, uncomfortable to be eating a meal out of doors. Leaning in around them were the too-young but recognizable faces of my Uncles Abe and Mel, their wives Gitl and Sylvia, Aunt Rochelle and her husband Manny Liebowitz, and my dad still a young kid making a clown-face for the camera. Off to the side and rear of the photo, barely in focus, stood Max's wife Ruth, and next to her a lean figure half-twisted away, his white face almost buried in a frenzied blast of uncombed hair and bristling unkempt beard, like Rasputin the Mad Monk.

That was Yossi.

If I had seen this picture, and been told about Yossi's role in our history, I might have spared us a family crisis that was quite painful, despite the absurdly trivial action that provoked it.

As it was, Yossi was so vague a figure in family lore that it had never occurred to me to ask why Max was "Uncle Max" while his younger brother was only "Cousin Yossi." Yet it's easy to understand why we might make that distinction. An uncle stands next to your father in respect and closeness of blood; a cousin may be as close as brother or sister, or distant by many removes. Max belonged to the same generation as all my other uncles. When my father's family assembled for the Passover Seder, Uncle Abe presided from the head of the table, but Uncle Max had the place of honor at Abe's right hand.

Whereas Yossi was "just a cousin," extremely removed. Only Uncle Max spoke of him as if he was or had been a living person. Every year when we sat down for the Seder, Max would remark, with a little edge in his voice, "Cousin Yossi sends his regards"— and no one would respond, as Uncle Abe scanned the opening prayers in the Haggadah and the other grown-ups fussily settled into their places.

# 1

Max and Abe were the sons of the brothers Isaac and Hershl Shpiglman, themselves the sons of the tailor Duvid Shpiglman who owned a shop just off the Cathedral Square in Zhitomir, a small city about ninety miles west of Kiev. Isaac was the older brother, Hershl three years younger. By the standards of the Pale of Settlement, Zhitomir had a large and thriving Jewish community. Nevertheless, the town experienced its share of the pogroms which periodically swept the Ukraine, when mobs (often instigated by agents of the Czar) stormed the Jewish districts to loot, burn, rape and murder.

Duvid Shpiglman taught his sons his trade, and on his death bequeathed them his shop and the good will of his customers; which the brothers shared until 1900, when Hershl Shpiglman, refusing a life forever menaced by the murderous impulses of his Christian

# Greenhorns

neighbors, emigrated to America with his wife Gitl and eight-year-old son Abe. He left behind his older brother Isaac, Isaac's wife Sarah and son Max—the fourth-born of their children, and the only one to survive infancy. But then, a year after Hershl's departure, the birth of another son, Yoisef who they called "Yossi," came as a last blessing to them.

Hershl Shpiglman prospered in the New World. At the start he, his wife and son Abe did piecework for a sweat-shop "cockroach," running three sewing machines in their tenement apartment on Orchard Street—what a name for an alley crammed with pushcart peddlers! They didn't pinch pennies—they *squeezed* them in a vice so hard that against all odds they wrung out enough spare cash to rent a tiny shop on Rivington Street. They painted on the window, in Yiddish, "Hershl Shpiglman Fine Tailoring."

Hershl's skill was equal to his boast. With an eye that could measure as finely as a razor cuts, with a hand that could snip and tuck and stitch and bend cloth to the elegant shapes conceived in his mind, he could make a hand-me-down suit look like Hart, Schaffner and Marx. That same sharp eye looked through the mere practice of his trade to understand its potential as a business. This is America, not Zhitomir! Why shouldn't the harried Jew on the Lower East Side dress himself as respectably as any Christian gentleman?

He scoured the warehouses where big clothiers dumped remaindered cloth and unwanted showroom samples, and haunted auctions and bankruptcy sales, buying up bolts of suiting, dress and shirtwaist material for pennies on the dollar—carried the goods to his shop where he created a line of ready-mades. People came. People bought. He rented a larger store, where the customer in his cast-offs and hand-me-downs could browse the racks like a connoisseur, pick out a suit, have it custom tailored by the owner himself or by his son Abraham, and walk away with a Fifth Avenue look for Hester Street prices. Quality goods and personal attention, in a *balabatish* atmosphere—a homelike Jewish establishment managed with intensely personal care.

# Richard Slotkin

In the midst of this labor of making and planning and earning and saving Hershl and Gitl also produced son Menashe and daughter Rokhl—Menashe who would change his name to Mel, Rokhl who would be called Rochelle. (Much later, when they were well past forty, a last son would be born to them, David, who became my father.) Nor did Hershl forget his brother Isaac, to whom he sent money orders along with pleas for Isaac to bring his family to the *goldene medinah.*

Then in 1905 there was a massive uprising in Russia following defeat in the Japanese War. Mobs marching on the Czar's palace in St. Petersburg were gunned down and hunted through the streets by Cossacks. Towns and cities erupted in violent strikes, peasants seized land in the countryside. Neither revolution nor repression spared the Jews. Peasants and workers enraged at the order which oppressed them would storm a police station one day and ravage the Jewish quarter the next. Cossacks bent on breaking the uprising turned their whips and sabers on the people whose denial of Christ was the ultimate insult to authority.

Hershl Shpiglman drained his till, and begged charity from his customers, to hire agents to find Isaac and his family and bring them forth from the Land of Egypt. They were finally located in Lvov, a Polish city under Austro-Hungarian rule, fully four hundred miles west of Zhitomir. The details of how they got there were never discussed. All I knew, as a child, was that it had been a harrowing journey that left them sick and shaken. And that Yossi, the four-year-old, had been lost for a time, given up for dead, then luckily—in some tellings "miraculously"—found again. In the end they were rescued, and the seal of their salvation was that sepia photograph, taken of the reunited family, in which the refugee Shpiglmans, having shed their immigrant rags, appeared in American dress alongside their Americanized kindred.

Hershl Shpiglman made his older brother partner in his store. But it was the younger brother, with his energy and his hard-won English, who really plied their trade. Isaac hid in the back, speaking

# Greenhorns

only Yiddish, cutting and stitching and pressing, avoiding the eyes of the customers. They might have gone on that way, but Hershl would never stand pat. He crossed the river to Brownsville, the Lower East Side's Brooklyn colony, plunged his savings and risked his credit to open a grand emporium on Pitkin Avenue. To shake off the Yiddish dust of Rivington Street, and suggest a kind of Bond Street distinction, he named it (in English) "Herschel's Fine Clothiers."

Once again, Isaac preferred to stay behind, enfolded in the ghetto's familiar, off-the-boat Jewishness.

But he failed to prosper. He became pious, in a way the Uncles (who were themselves strictly observant) considered excessive and unworldly. He neglected the business, and although Hershl kept lending him cash, his store went bust and he went back to operating a sweatshop sewing machine, coughing wetly, his lungs ruined by floating lint and fetid air. Tante Sarah became sickly, "a nervous wreck." Together they withered like uprooted plants. Their son Max had health and energy; but he spent it in bad company, went on the bum, joined the army, became a Communist—what didn't he do? He'd send money home, but it was never enough. The younger child, Yossi, was plagued by a lingering nervous debility contracted during their flight. What it added up to was a steep decline into failure and death. Isaac and Sarah died in 1927, and Yossi disappeared into a series of "institutions," some of which seemed to be jails, others hospitals.

The Uncles were shamefaced discussing the ruin of Isaac's family. Of Isaac himself they only said: "He had no head for business." Of Tante Sarah: she was a frail woman who let her emotions run away with her. Of Max they said: "A young man's faults—a good heart in spite of everything." Then what destroyed the family? No one wanted to say it, because how can you blame such things on a child who can't help himself? So they talked in circles around what they truly believed: that Yossi was the family's curse, a problem child who sucked the life out of his suffering parents.

# Richard Slotkin

As if the angelic little boy in the sepia photograph had somehow transformed into the Angel of Death.

I can't say that I took this story, and its dark implications, to heart. Uncle Isaac, Tante Sarah and Cousin Yossi were not real people to me, just figures in a sad folk tale. Apart from the sepia photograph, Uncle Max was the only proof I had that these misfortunates had ever lived. But Max rarely referred to his parents, and as far as I knew only spoke Yossi's name that one time every year, when (as we sat down at the Seder table) he would tell the company, "Cousin Yossi sends his regards."

But no one ever asked Max to return the courtesy. So I supposed it was just one of Uncle Max's little jokes—because needling Uncle Abe was his favorite indoor sport, and for me the highlight of our Seder.

2

My father's family celebrated Passover in the East Flatbush town house Zeydeh bought in 1926, when his business began to prosper and the neighborhood was new. After my grandmother's death, Uncle Abe and Aunt Gitl moved in to take care of the old man. When Zeydeh died, Abe became Chairman of the Board in a double sense: president of the company and head of the family. He was a wealthy man, who could have bought himself a bigger house in a better neighborhood. But he honored his father with all his heart. So he stayed in Zeydeh's house; and although "Herschel's Fine Clothiers, Ltd." was now a national brand, with franchises in major cities, Abe still went to work every weekday at the "flagship" store—a fancy name for the often-refurbished "emporium" on Pitkin Avenue—and descended from his office to personally attend to long-time customers. It was a device of magic: as long as he maintained, on the old ground, his father's tradition of quality workmanship and personal attention, the modern company would preserve the reputation his father had won for it.

Uncle Abe's well-cut suits graced the comfortable round belly he called his "corporation." His pink cheeks were so cleanly shaved they looked polished. His scanty hair was slicked back tight to his round head, his nimble thick-fingered hands were always scrubbed and his nails manicured. He spoke with a heavy Yiddish accent. Until he was eight he had lived in Zhitomir, and even after the move to New York Yiddish was the preferred language at home and in the shop. In Abe's own house nothing but American was spoken. He named his son Sherman (which Abe pronounced "Shuyman"), inspired by the bronze equestrian statue of the American general which faced the Plaza Hotel on Fifth Avenue. Yet he kept rigorously kosher and attended synagogue on the Sabbath and all the Holy Days, including Simkhas Torah and Tisha B'Av. The Seders over which he presided seemed to go on forever. It was not enough to bless and expound the Passover, the unleavened bread, the bitter herbs; we had to consider Rabbi Gamaliel's opinion on this and Rabbi Akiva's interpretation of that and the commentary of Rashi on the other—while rich odors of roasting chicken, braised beef and browned onions from Aunt Gitl's kitchen tormented me all through the endless postponement of dinner.

Abe would sit at the head of the Seder table, and Aunt Gitl at the foot—closest to the kitchen. Our families would take their places around the table following a protocol set by Zeydeh, modified by Abe.

Sherman had the seat to his father's left. He was fair-haired, stocky and full of energy, mildly impatient for his elders to leave the business in his capable hands. His wife Tessie was a dead ringer for Bess Myerson, the Jewish Miss America. Their daughter Bonnie was an aspiring diva, who had sung the Star-Spangled Banner at Ebbets Field on Opening Day—though the ads her father bought on Dodgers radio might have had something to do with it.

Uncle Mel had the place next to Sherman. His look was a glare, his lips pursed as if tasting something foul. While Zeydeh was alive Mel was second to Abe in the business; now that Abe was in charge, he was second to Sherman. He proved himself the better man by being harsher in his judgments, stricter in the conduct of business, rigidly correct in all things. In his household his word was the Law. His wife Sylvia must make up and dress as if for dinner just to go to the A & P. His daughter must marry a doctor. His son Harold must become a CPA.

Harold instead became a high school math teacher. He could not have done greater outrage to his father's self-worth if he had proclaimed himself a bastard. Mel cut him off, declared him dead, sat *shiva* for him.

Only Abe came to the *shiva*—Abe, grieving for his nephew Harold, shamed by his stiff-necked idiot brother, but worried that this brother, who was now cut off from his child, might also be rejected by his kindred.

The rest of the family reacted with shame, anger and superstitious fear at Mel's gratuitous summoning of the Angel of Death. Nevertheless, we were careful to exclude Harold from any occasion to which Mel and Sylvia had to be invited. So Harold's absence haunted all the major occasions of family life—weddings, bar mitzvahs, funerals, and Abe's Seder—another little man who wasn't there.

My dad and Mel did not like each other. The thirteen-year age difference was only part of the problem. Mel disapproved my father's very existence, which was shameful evidence that in their old age his parents, who were already Bubby and Zeydeh, were still tangling up the sheets at night. Also, my dad taught high school English. An obscure chain of thought and emotion led Mel to blame my father's example for tempting Harold to betray him, and he took my father's presence at the Seder as criticism of Harold's exclusion. Mel refused to look at my dad, which probably put a kink in his neck because Mel and Sylvia always sat across from our family down at Aunt Gitl's end of the table.

Next up toward the head of the table on our side would be Aunt Rochelle and her husband Manny, a chiropractor. They were always a little uneasy, because they suspected the Uncles discounted chiropractic as a medical profession. They weren't wrong.

# Greenhorns

Uncle Max had the seat of honor on Abe's right. Age had something to do with it—after Abe, Max was the oldest. Also, by honoring Max, Abe reminded us of Zeydeh's love for his brother Isaac. And then—of all the Uncles, Abe and Max were the only ones born in Zhitomir, the only ones who knew by experience the darkness of that place, and the only ones who knew what it was to be a greenhorn in America.

Every year Max and Abe carried on a bantering duel. Abe took his Haggadah straight. Max pitched in sarcastic commentaries on God's peculiar sense of justice, massacring first-born infants and for the sins of the fathers cursing a whole generation to perish in the desert. Abe conducted the service in Hebrew. Max spoke his portion in Yiddish: *"Das iz di broyt fun tsores. . . ."* (This is the bread of affliction.) Thus we were reminded that while Abe and his children had learned Judaism and Hebrew in Talmud Torah, Max sent his children to the Sholom Aleichem School, where they studied Marxist dialectics in Yiddish.

Max was the classic odd-man-out uncle, a well-beloved pain in the ass. Abe, Mel and Sherman were successful businessmen, and dressed the part. Max was an organizer for the Amalgamated Clothing Workers of America, and his idea of dress-up was a battered sports jacket and Western string tie—the jacket defiantly bought at a consignment shop rather than Herchel's Fine Clothiers, Ltd. He had a face like a leather bag packed tight with rocks, his chin a sharp wedge, his nose cracked in the middle and slanting sideways, nails battered rather than manicured, hair a mess of uncombed waves. He was long-limbed but big in the shoulders, a classic welterweight's build. In fact, as a young man he had boxed in that class at the local Maccabee Club—not exactly the after-school activity of a good Jewish boy.

But then, Max was *not* a good Jewish boy. I learned his history in bits and pieces, much of it from disparaging remarks by Abe, Mel and Sherman. But what they saw as disreputable was to me a kind of Jewish swashbuckling.

# Richard Slotkin

While Max's father was sinking deeper into failure and piety, Max had gone native. He roved the mean streets of the Lower East Side with a mixed gang of Jews, Poles and Italians, shoplifted and ran numbers for barbershop wise-guys, pitched pennies and played handball against the brick walls of the tenement, chalked skelly courts on the sidewalk and made book on the contest. Starting when he was twelve Max haunted the gym at the Maccabee Club, where a Jewish bantamweight with cauliflower ears taught him how to box. He fought in clubs, first as a bantam then as a welterweight, and lost at least as often as he won. At age sixteen he went on the bum and rode the rails all the way out to the Coast and back, jumping off to find work as a ranch- or farm-hand, odd-job man, navvie on the Embarcadero. In 1917 he enlisted in the army, fought in France with the American Expeditionary Forces, and was discharged as a platoon sergeant.

Sherman—exasperated by my hero-worship—described the next of Max's derelictions: "It's not enough he has to make the world safe for democracy while his family goes broke. When he gets back he has to become a Communist. And while he saves the world again for the working class his brother goes to the nut house and his parents die of grief. Zeydeh says to him, 'Who do you think you are, President Wilson? History is to you a personal insult?'"

But becoming a Communist was the seal of Max's Americanization. He had seen the country, he had fought for it. It was his. So if it needed a push that there should be justice for the working class, it was his job to push it. If the Red Squad came after him, so be it. However, he was (as Aunt Ruth told me) "a wonderful comrade but a lousy Communist." Dialectical materialism made as little sense to him as Talmud and Midrash. He had his own understanding of how history worked, learned in the prize-ring and the trenches. He tore up his Party card and started over as an organizer for the Amalgamated Clothing Workers—a calling in which he would spend the rest of his life.

Max himself made little of his adventures. He would tell funny stories about the boxcar etiquette of penniless hoboes, or the half-baked schemes of barber-shop hustlers conniving to bilk each other of nickels and dimes. But he was frustratingly reticent about the things I most wanted to know. When I was eight, and afraid of schoolyard bullies, I asked would he teach me to box. "You don't need to box. What you need is how to fight. And for that—you find the wolf you got inside, and let it loose." When I asked what wolf he meant, he grinned. "If it's there, you'll find it." He had worked on a ranch in Wyoming. "Were you a cowboy?" I asked him. "Did you ride a horse?" He gave me a look: "Riding horses is for Cossacks. I walked behind with a pitchfork and threw hay into a wagon." Once or twice I tried to ask him about being a soldier in the First War. He would smile and ruffle my hair, and look apologetic. "It's not a thing to talk about, boychik." He refused to present himself as a model for anyone to follow. In this he deferred to the values of my other uncles.

But he bridled at their put-down of his motives for enlisting in the army and for becoming a Communist. "You think history is not your business? One day it will come looking for you. If you don't take it personally, you won't know what hit you."

His wife Ruth was just his type. She had dark olive skin like a gypsy, wore absolutely no makeup, her kinky hair barely restrained by a colorful head-scarf. Back in the '30s Uncle Abe as an act of kindness had hired her to keep the books for the Manhattan store. She proceeded to organize the shop and win recognition by the NLRB. Their son Daniel was now a lawyer for the UAW in Detroit, daughter Susan a social worker in Pittsburgh.

In this gathering I had had a favored place. My superior schoolwork was the cue for extravagant expectations of future honors accruing to the family name. In 1962 that expectation seemed to blossom into Jackie-Robinson-like achievement, when I won a graduate fellowship in American history at Yale University. This was not merely "an out-of-town school" like Syracuse or Penn State. It was the Ivy League, which was as exclusive, and as closed to Jews, as any Greenwich or Scarsdale country club. Yet these aristocrats were actually *paying* me to take their classes! The prestige of a "Ph.D. college professor" was not as self-evident as that of a lawyer, physician or accountant. But if you thought about it (and my aunts and uncles did) it had an air of high culture that more than compensated.

To mark my readiness for this new stage of life I did what few students at Brooklyn College then dared—I grew a beard.

The American folk music revival had begun while I was in high school. My friends and I bought guitars or banjos, and learned to play a mix of blue-grass, political songs and traditional blues by listening to old 78s and Folkways reissues of Bill Monroe, Woody Guthrie, Leadbelly, and the Almanac Singers. Weekend mornings we'd sling our instruments, hop the IRT subway from Brooklyn to Bleecker Street, and join the throng around the fountain in Washington Square Park. If you got there early enough you could play a set and gather an audience, maybe even catch the ear of Dave Van Ronk or Pete Seeger.

Van Ronk was my Man. He could pick a guitar like Billy-be-damned, and his rasping vocals had the authentic growl of the blues. Van Ronk had a beard, a classic hipster's mustache-and-goatee. Reason enough for me to grow one.

In those days sporting a beard set you up for insults by "regular Americans" of every class and creed, from college presidents ("Beatniks!") to construction workers ("Hippies!"), to the odorous wino on the subway who sneered at me as "a fine young gen'lman with a beard." So I was prepared for my parents' dismay, and for disapproval from the rest of the family when we gathered for the first-night Seder.

Instead when I walked through the door Uncle Abe's apple cheeks turned the purple of apoplexy, words exploded in him too thick and fast to get out of his mouth in good order. "You! What! What! You come in here? You—like a greenhorn?"

Every one froze—as you do when you hear from the street outside the smash and glass-metal crump of a car crash.

# Greenhorns

Only Abe was alive, his eyes bulging with outrage, his smooth round cheeks beet-red. "Like a greenhorn!" he cried. "To come in my house with a beard like a greenhorn!"

Of all the names a beard could call down, "greenhorn" was the last I expected. And to be called greenhorn by *this* man? With his fresh-off-the-boat Yiddish accent and his Hester Street religion? I nearly laughed in his face.

The worst, most nearly unforgiveable thing I could possibly have done.

From which I was saved by Aunt Gitl and Sherman and Aunt Rochelle, who swarmed around Abe, shushing and trying to calm him.

Abe appealed to Aunt Gitl. "To spit on us! To spit on everything!" He was wide-eyed, bewildered, she must explain how this thing could have happened!

Sherman stepped in, shielding his father's face from my view. "Poppa," he said, "for chrissake it's just a beard!" Meaning: *Stop embarrassing yourself!*

My cheeks were burning, but I was glad I hadn't laughed at him. Uncle Abe was hurt, even if I had no idea why, and as angry and mortified as I was I didn't want to make it worse.

Uncle Mel glared at my father. "You never gave respect to this family," he said. "From the first you thought you were better than the rest of us."

My dad has no temper at all—it's a measure of how hot the situation was that he snapped back: "This from a man who throws away his only son."

And in the midst of this storm, Uncle Max stepped in and took Abe's arm. "Abe! Let it be! Don't make a craziness about nothing."

"You think it's not an insult?" Abe's face was still flushed, but now he spread his hands, inviting Max to save him from his distress.

"What insult?" Max spoke soothingly: "It's just a beard."

Abe and Max looked at each other for a silent moment. Max

nodded, as if acknowledging a shared understanding. "We know from beards, Avrom. But this is just an American beard. On an American face."

Then my mom slapped her hands together like a teacher calling the kindergarten to order. "Oh be quiet all of you! Abe my dear? I love you with all my heart, but watch the mouth you open! This is my son, not some bum off the street. If he wants a beard he can grow it, without asking your permission." (This after she'd spent two days begging me to shave it off.)

"Please," said Aunt Gitl, "it's *yontiff*. Let's sit, and read our Haggadah, and soon we'll eat."

So we sat. Uncle Abe led us through the ceremony, but without his usual verve. Max raised an eyebrow now and again, but refrained from needling him. Then we ate, but the table talk, which usually ran up and down the emotional and decibel scale, was soft and even. The explosion had left us all slightly deafened, all sounds were muffled.

This quiet meal was the armistice. Overnight there would be a cooling-off period. In the morning the diplomats would begin the work of reconciliation.

# 3

Uncle Abe's ambassador was his son Sherman, who stopped by our apartment in the late morning. Mom set out coffee and macaroons, and after a bite and a sip Sherman came round to the object of his visit. He wished to offer an "explanation" of his father's behavior—to say "apology" would be to magnify what had happened, when the point was to diminish it.

He had his work cut out for him. The more I thought about what happened, the more it got under my skin. That Uncle Abe should humiliate me in front of the whole family! If I had insulted him, yes—but he had no right, my uncle not my father, to rebuke me for what was none of his business. "He called me a name," I said, "and he meant it as an insult."

# Greenhorns

Sherman shrugged. "Michael," he said, "you have to understand my Pop. It's a different generation. A beard doesn't mean to him what it means to you—not that I know what it means to you, but you're young, right? So you just do things. But my Pop? The beard reminds him of all the trouble on account of Uncle Isaac and Cousin Yossi." Sherman needed me to appreciate just how hard it had been during those years, when Abe was torn between the compelling needs of their business and Zeydeh's determination to save his brother Isaac from ruin. "Zeydeh and Pop were building a business from nothing, like a man building a staircase up into the sky with no guarantee there's a floor above to anchor to. One bad mistake and they're falling through the air." Yet time and again Zeydeh would give money they could not really spare to help Uncle Isaac. And all for nothing!

Sherman leaned in—this was the point. "The truth is Uncle Isaac became a religious nut. Praying and conferring with the rebbes while the customers are left hanging. In Russia they pay you to study Midrash. In America you have to earn your living." Abe begged Zeydeh to stop throwing good money after bad. But Zeydeh wouldn't face what his brother had become. "A shrug, a sigh, 'My brother! He's got no head for business.'"

Sherman's eyes lost focus, as if he was seeing an image somewhere behind me. "No head for business? He let his hair and beard grow out—like one of these Hasidim you see that don't speak English. The first time I saw him, I was just a little kid, he scared the crap out of me. Hair sprouting from everywhere, hanging from under his cap, eyebrows like haystacks, a dirty tangled beard down his whole front like a bib, hair sprouting out his nose and his ears like you see on old bums that don't take care of themselves."

"Wait a minute," I said, "you mean my Uncle Abe treats me like an enemy because I remind him of Uncle Isaac?"

Sherman shook his head. "Enemy? No, you don't understand." He gave me a straight look, man to man. "He yelled at you because you frightened him."

"With a beard?"

"Not just the beard." Sherman looked at my dad. "Uncle Dave, you remember . . ." Nephew and uncle were nearly the same age, the son of Abe and Gitl's youth and the son of Bubby and Zeydeh's old age.

My father nodded. "I was only at their apartment once or twice—then I wouldn't go. It was the smell."

"Like they never left Russia," Sherman declared. "No matter what we did for them, they kept sliding backwards. Uncle Isaac was useless. Tante Sarah was *meshugga*—and why not, with a husband out of this world, one son on the bum and the other out of his mind."

"I understand about Uncle Isaac," I said. "What's Cousin Yossi got to do with anything?"

Sherman suddenly blushed, and gave my father a look. My dad shrugged. "We never talk about him either."

Sherman was annoyed. Why should *he* have to be the one to explain? "You want the story, ask Max. But I'll tell you this: Yossi was at the bottom of their craziness. The kid had problems. They went through hell getting out of Russia, and the story was the kid got lost—days, weeks, who knows how long it actually was? But they found him again. That's the point: they found him again. He was four years old. Sure it's scary for a little kid. Nightmares, hanging on to Mama for dear life. But kids get over things. You just keep telling them there's no monsters under the bed. Eventually they outgrow it."

Sherman shook his head. "But Uncle Isaac and Tante Sarah made a whole superstition of it. 'A miracle,' Uncle Isaac would say—grab you by the shirt and stare in your eyes, 'A miracle a miracle.' Like finding Moses in the bulrushes. Then Yossi starts having these moods and tantrums, and Tante Sarah starts screaming it's not really Yossi, it's a changeling, a dybbuk. From Orchard Street they ran right back to the Middle Ages! And the praying, and the repenting, one rabbi after another—this one says sacrifice a chicken, that one says give him a *schvitz* in the steam-bath, another one sets *bankes* on his belly, hot suction cups to pull the bad spirit out. All they did was pound the kid's craziness back into his brain, till he believed his own *meshuggass*."

Sherman looked to my dad for support. "You remember, Uncle Dave. The things he'd say. Yossi. You'd be sitting at the table, eating a meal, he sits there like a dummy. Then all of a sudden out of nowhere he leans over to me, like we're having a conversation, and says, 'There are dead people in the trees.' I'm what—ten years old? 'Where" I ask him, 'what trees?' scared shitless. He looks at me like *I'm* crazy. 'All of them' he says.

"So he has a nervous breakdown. The head-shrinkers get hold of him, pump him full of dope and shoot him with electricity. He goes in the hospital, he comes out, he goes back . . . a dozen times. This way he kills his mother and father. When they're gone he starts on the rest of us. In the end even Max had to agree. Enough is enough. So we sent Yossi to that hospital upstate." He glanced at me: "You want more, go ask Max. He still goes up there to see Yossi once a month. My dad stopped going years ago. The lights are on there, but nobody's home."

Which was how I got the astonishing news that Yossi was real, and was still alive.

## 4

Uncle Max and Aunt Ruth had a two-bedroom apartment in the Amalgamated Clothing Workers cooperative housing project just north of the Lower East Side. Max and Ruth lived in the Dwellings, the original buildings at the heart of the expanding complex, an enclave of modest six-story units in two tones of brick surrounding a park with tree-shaded benches and playgrounds for the children. Each building held a library, a gym, a nursery and an assembly hall. Art-deco friezes decorated the entries, reflecting the aesthetics of the early 1930s and the union's dream of housing workers well and beautifully.

# Richard Slotkin

Max had agreed to talk with me about Yossi on one condition: that I come with him next time he drove up to visit Yossi at Rockland State Hospital. To tell the truth, I hesitated. One look at Yossi had "scared the crap" out of Sherman and my dad when they were kids, and everyone else in the family was afraid even to mention his name lest it conjure his terrible image. I accepted Max's condition the way you take a dare you are ashamed to refuse.

We had first to enjoy a meal together—slices of roast chicken, kasha and green beans, with glasses of seltzer and cherry soda. Then Ruth sanctioned the shift to business. "So," she grinned, "who do you think was more embarrassed? You, or your Uncle Abe?"

"You mean, 'who was angrier.'" I said.

"Please," she said. "The anger was from embarrassment. For both of you. You understood that. It's why you didn't open a mouth at him."

"Maybe."

"You frightened him," said Max, "so he let himself loose. Then he was ashamed everyone should see." He thought for a moment. "He's like a man on a tightrope, Abe. On the one side is his father—his belief in the God of Israel, his care for his family, his way of doing business. This Abe loves, he's born to this. But it's from the world of greenhorns. And on the other side is the world 'America,' with success and prosperity and that all of us should be safe here, to live among the Americans as if we were one of them. He walks the tightrope between these worlds, balancing—shaky. Then a nephew rises up in his face with a beard like a greenhorn—he loses his balance, he's falling through the air without a net. So he yells at you to put himself right again."

Max's version made sense to me. It jibed with Sherman's explanation, and took it a little deeper. It also occurred to me that Uncle Mel must have had similar anxieties—and saved his own balance by throwing his son Harold off the tightrope. But then there was Max. "So what about you?" I said. "You come from the same place."

# Greenhorns

Max shrugged. "I fell off the tightrope."

Ruth gave him a look: "Fell? You jumped!"

Which made Max laugh. "For me it was easier. My father was no example to live up to, not like Zeydeh. And after what happened with Yossi I had no use for the religion." He glanced at Ruth, then sat up straight. "All right. Let me show you what everyone is afraid of."

He picked up a photo album which had been set on the empty chair next to him in preparation for my visit. He opened it to a book-marked page and turned it for me to see.

This was my first sight of that 1930 picnic photograph, with Bubby and Zeydeh on the bench surrounded by their older married children, and my pre-teen dad mugging for the camera—and off to the side Ruth tending the wraith-like figure whose pale cheeks and forehead were nearly devoured by the ravenous hair that sprouted wildly from his head and poured down his chest in bristling waves. Cousin Yossi.

"Abe sees you with a beard," said Max, "this is what he sees. He's our nightmare, this Yossi. He's what America couldn't save. So maybe if we stop scraping our cheeks and slicking our hair down, the *Yossi* will sprout out of our heads and our faces for all the goyim to see."

Ruth leaned across the table and covered his hand with her own. "But he doesn't scare you," she said.

"No," said Max, "because I understand my brother Yossi." He looked straight at me. "And I want you to understand him. So he won't be a nightmare to you also."

This is the story Max told me:

# 5

"He was a little golden baby, Yossi, with hair like the yellow down on a baby chick, and as soon as he could walk he used to chase after me on his little short legs, giggling the whole time. Of everything in life my mother loved Yossi best. I felt the same. He was my baby

# Richard Slotkin

brother. We had a lot of fun together. Even my friends didn't mind him tagging along. He had a head full of notions that would make you laugh to hear them: 'The sun's like peaches, it gets ripe in the summer and falls off the tree in the winter.' Forget the crazy face in the photograph, and picture that.

"Then picture in your head Zhitomir—it's not some rag-gedy-pants *shtetl* out in the sticks, it's a small city like New Rochelle or White Plains. And the Jews? Not like America, where we're the fly in the milk pail. Half the city is Jewish. Half the holy places, half the businesses, more than half the schools. Jews, Russians, and Ukraines, we're in each other's face every day. We smell each other's breath. As boys we all played together, swam and fished in the river and threw rocks at the swells when they rode through the streets in their carriages.

"Back then my dad was not especially pious. He kept kosher and observed the Sabbath and went to synagogue on the High Holidays like everyone else. But to argue Talmud or muse upon the ways and purposes of the Almighty was as foreign as Einstein to him. He wore then a suit with a vest and trimmed his beard short, same as the Russian tradesmen. He liked things to stay always the same—mealtimes, work time, the way things were arranged in the shop. Keep the world steady. Don't jostle it, it might collapse on you. My mother was the same, except more nervous—one eye always on the window afraid what might be outside.

"This is our ordinary life. But in that life a shift of the wind, a word from the Czar, and the mobs will come roaring through the streets in pogrom. So we had ourselves a defense, a set of tough boys trained by Jacob Shuster, a Jew that served in the Russian army and by his wits and strength lived to be discharged. And we had a plan: if the worst happens, run to the Old Synagogue in the heart of the Jewish quarter, where the narrow twisted streets will be barricaded.

"In 1905, in the spring, you could smell trouble. But all the same, every day is just another day, Jews and Russkies and Ukraines face to face, buying and selling—shoes and fish and shirts and hats and bread. Why should something happen this day rather than another? And if it happens (*when* it happens), why in Zhitomir rather than Odessa or Kishiniev?

"So on a day in May we start off for school as usual. I'm nine years old. We head up the street that runs through the Jewish quarter, then turns a corner and runs to the Cathedral Square. I'm marching up front with my gang, heading for the state school where everyone went, Jews and non-Jews, to study history and mathematics and Russian. Behind us—the little ones, Yossi and the rest, skipping along, Yossi holding hands with a little girl Shana that was his special friend, heading for the Jewish school over by the New Synagogue. They had there what over here we call a kindergarten.

"Then at a certain point the little ones turn left up a small side street to the New Synagogue, and the big ones right to the Russian school. As I turn away I look back. Yossele waves his hand at me—and he throws me a look, a little wide in the eyes as if he's afraid to be going off without me. That look comes back to me now—but to tell the truth, it was exactly the same look he always gave me when we parted ways for school. Only now, after, does it have a meaning.

"We're almost to the school when Misha Zenko, a Christian boy that was friends to us, comes yelling, 'Turn around! Get out! They're coming for you!'

"I turn and run back the way I came, thinking *I have to get Yossi,* snatch him out of the kinder school and race him back to the Old Synagogue where the Defenders will be throwing up their barricades. But it's too late. The mob is already turning the corner up from the Cathedral Square, a half-dozen police on horses quick-trotting ahead of the mass, behind them the priests in their tall hats, bearing gold icons of their saints on long poles, chanting in that weird holy-Russian language, then the teamsters banging their whip-handles on the ground like drumbeats, and behind them the mob howling and crying out, waving rifles and shotguns and scythes and long clubs. So I duck back, and dodge my way through the little side streets, saying to myself that Yossi's teachers are grown-ups, they know what to do, they'll gather the kids and rush them safe behind the barricades.

"But when I get to the barricades Yossi isn't there—none of the kids from the cheder are there. Everyone swarms around me, talking all at once, where is this one, where is that one? My mother comes pushing through the crowd and grabs me and gives me a shake that makes my teeth rattle: 'Where's Yossi? Where's Yossi?'

"I tell her what happened, but she doesn't listen: 'You lost him? You lost your brother and left him out there?' She shakes me and shakes me till Papa gets hold of her and makes her stop. What could I say to her? That Yossi went left and I went right, the same as always, and so I came back but he. . . ? *Not my fault!* I thought, *What could I have done different?*

"Then I said to myself: 'That's a stupid question. This happened. The question is, what can you do about it?'

"All that night we crouch behind the barricades and listen to the pogrom howling and singing in our streets, see the fires burst up here and there, hear shooting. Two, three times the mob makes to rush the barricade. Shuster and his pals drive them off with a few gunshots. A mob is a bully, and a bully is a coward.

"Next morning, before the sun comes up—gray sky, the streets gray with the smoke drifting—Shuster and some of the Defenders are going out to look for the ones left behind, especially the children from the cheder. I tell Shuster, 'Take me with you.' 'You're too young.' 'If Yossi's hiding, he won't come out. But if he hears my voice. . . .'

"So he takes me with him into the streets, doors broken in, windows smashed, bodies lying like garbage in the gutter. We get to the cheder—it's a shell, burnt out. A smell like a horrible meat, burning. I call for Yossi, but there's nothing. We rummage the streets all around, 'Yossi! Yossele!' Nothing.

"In the silence we hear the priests ranting in the Cathedral Square, the whip-handles drumming the ground, a sound like wind of the mob howling in response.

# Greenhorns

"We go back to the barricade, and Shuster tells all those mothers and fathers the truth. Nobody found, they must all be dead. Screaming—of course, what else? My mother—tries to claw her face off, they have to hold her hands. But there is no time for this. They'll be coming after us again as soon as the priests have finished. There was a bridge over the river behind us, still open. The Defenders will hold the barricade—everyone else should make a run for it. I ask Shuster, let me stay. Shooting those people with a gun would ease my heart. 'Take care of your people, boychik,' he says. 'You have plenty of time yet to get killed.' The last I saw he was leaning against the barricade, cleaning his rifle barrel with a rag and a long stick, whistling.

"So we ran for it—and once we started there was no stopping. It's four hundred miles from Zhitomir to Lvov. It took us three months to get there, watching every step every minute of every day, not knowing whether to turn left or turn right, thinking, studying, arguing, trying to guess which way was safe, which way They might be waiting for us, begging food—guessing whether this town would feed us, or that one to the north. Four hundred miles like that. Not every grown man or woman had the strength to go on.

"Yossi was not yet five years old, so he could not be alive—could not be. Of course there was no certainty. But each day of this new living, these fears and thinkings, this watching the steps of our feet, this piling up of days and distance—these *made* him dead, and every day buried him deeper. Three months. Four hundred miles. Even my mother gave up grieving and fell into mourning. Yossi was dead. Yossi was dead. The little golden chickie boy.

"We get across the border into Austrian Polish territory—a shanty-town on the outskirts of Lvov. There are thousands of us, swarming, nothing to eat. We sneak into town to beg bread in the streets and the Austrian cops run us out. So we go to the garbage dump to pick through the *dreck* of the city for rotten fruit and shriveled greens and bones to make a soup. This too takes care and watching, to find the good bits among all that crap, to spot the

145

bully-boys who watch for you to make a find, then beat you up and steal it. And one morning I find a big knuckle of beef-bone with a cap of grizzle and fat—snatch it up quick and spin my head around to see if the bully-boys spotted me.

"And there is Yossi. With a peel of orange in his little hand.

"He has come back to me from *Death.*

"I'm choking. I have to scream!

"He just looks up at me. His face is black with filth, scratched all over. He doesn't say a word. Just looks.

"I grab him, I lift him. He's alive! 'Yossi,' I cry, 'Yossi where were you? We thought we lost you!'

"Yossi says: 'He wasn't lost.' Not crying, not excited. Just saying. Maybe putting it a strange way—but at such a moment who can pick his words?"

Max stopped speaking. He looked off away from me, as if he was watching a movie playing on the wall behind me.

Then he looked at me again. "You can imagine the scene when I brought him back. My mother and father—the shrieking, the crying, the yelling, 'My God, a miracle! Is it Yossi? How can it be! Is it really you?' They ask me how I found him, but don't wait for an answer. 'It's Yossi! How did you live, Yossi? How did you get here?'

"Not waiting for him to answer.

"And in the middle of that storm of tears and words he sits *shtum.* Little kids—they know their parents are always making a fuss about something. So they let Mom and Dad carry on, blah blah blah, when it's done they go about their business. I thought, maybe that's how it is with Yossi. Maybe in his little head the time he was away becomes nothing now that he's back.

"Everyone in camp was awe-struck by the incredible fact of Yossi's reappearance. 'A miracle of God!' What else would you call it? How else could you imagine it? We became famous, thousands of hopeless wishes sprang to life out of our miracle: 'If God can choose the Shpiglmans, why not us? Are we less pious, less deserving?'

# Greenhorns

"My father embraced the miracle as a drowning man seizes a log of wood. After all that had happened, we were still in God's hands! Yossi was the proof! He brought Yossi before the Kehillah, the council of rabbis in Lvov, and they affirmed Yossi's existence as *nisimdik*, miraculous. My father began to think of himself as a holy man, to whom God had entrusted a prodigy. His beard had grown out full during our flight; now he refused to trim it, and wore always an embroidered skull-cap one of the rabbis gave him.

"I don't blame him. The miracle gave us the strength to go on. Who had the time—who had the courage—to notice there was something not right with Yossi? You're clinging to the edge of a cliff by one fingernail—you don't question how can such a thing be, you just close your eyes and hold on. The world spun around and sped us forward. A few weeks later the agent sent by Uncle Hershl found us, bringing money and steamship tickets, and setting our feet on the path to the New World. In a rush we went from Lvov to the steerage, from the steerage to the dock, from the dock to the embrace of Uncle Hershl and his family, from the embrace to the apartment on Orchard Street and the shop Uncle Hershl would share with my father.

"Then finally we could stop and breathe and look around, and pay attention to each other. We had bread, and the love of family, we were safe in a new world—but now it was impossible not to see that Yossi was becoming more and more strange.

"He would play and laugh the same as he used to do. Then in the middle stop still, and stand silent, his eyes glazed over, like ice on a pond. Strange sudden sayings popped out of his mouth: 'They don't give you eat.' 'The man was inside out.' While we were eating, he would suddenly stop and stare and say, 'He wasn't lost.' Or 'He don't get eat.'

"Never '*I* wasn't lost'—always '*He*.' It made your head spin to figure out what he meant. That it wasn't himself, it was the rest of us who were lost? Or was he thinking of someone else entirely, someone who was with him at cheder or on the long trek from Zhitomir to Lvov? Or was he two minds in one body, one that was lost and another that wasn't? It was like looking into a mirror with another mirror behind you, and you see a million reflections of your face getting smaller and smaller as if you are sliding backwards down a bottomless hole.

"Mama became more and more frantic. She spun like a top between grabbing and hugging him, and twisting away from him in fear and disgust. She'd beg him, 'Yossele my child, please be *good*!' But he was already being good, if by good you mean not making a mess and getting into trouble. It was his silence, his still-ness, his eyes like a dead fish that tore at her nerves, unbearable, and when she couldn't take any more she'd swoop on him like a hawk, clutching and crying and kissing and begging him to *Stop!*

"Stop what? He already turned off the light and closed the shop.

"Eventually he had to go to school. The first days in the class-room the teachers thought he was a gift from God—sits in his seat, doesn't talk out of turn . . . doesn't talk, period. Then the teacher reads the children the story of "Three Little Pigs"—and Yossi starts screaming at her "Pigs eat dead people! Pigs eat dead people!"

So they send him home to sit in Mama's kitchen like a clay go-lem and she tip-toes around him, trembling. And one day he walks into the kitchen and stands and looks at her calmly and says, 'The trees are full of dead people.'

"She shrieks at him he's tearing out her heart!

"My father comes running and tries to calm her. It's a miracle Yossi is here, we should be grateful! She turns on him as well. It was no miracle, never a miracle. The 'Yossi' God sent back was not the true Yossi. The true Yossi was the light of her life, a beautiful baby given to her after she suffered miscarriages and babies dead of cholera—he was a sunbeam, a happy frisky little boy with a head full of questions and a mouth full of words. The 'Yossi' they found in the garbage was cold and dead inside, a dybbuk, a horror in the shape of her sweet baby!

# Greenhorns

"My parents. They still thought God was in charge of the whole operation—so if Yossi wasn't a miracle, he was a curse.

"But I was there from the start and I saw no miracle. And no dybbuk either, except maybe in my *mother's* head, that she should refuse to recognize her own child. Because he was not always babbling craziness or sitting *shtum* like corpse. Sometimes he would give me quickly a *look*. As if to say: '*We* know, don't we? *We* know what has happened.' In such moments he was Yossi again, my baby brother."

Max became still. He dropped his eyes and looked at his own hands folded on the table. With an effort he raised up and looked at me again.

"For me that was the worst. Because what did I know? That on the day of the pogrom I turned right and Yossi turned left. After that only Yossi knows what happened, and he won't say—or he can't. Somehow he got away when the mob stormed the cheder. Maybe he was found by other Jews who fled by a different way—they feed him but don't keep their eye on him, so he gets lost again, and picked up again, and so on. That much we can guess.

"But try to imagine how it *was* for him being lost. He expects his Mama and Papa, or his big brother, will come for him. But day after day we don't come. What happens inside him when he finally knows we're not coming? How does he ask for help? Does he pick someone and plead, or just scream at the world? And when it goes on and on, and that's all his life is—how does he keep going forward? But of course he isn't going 'forward,' he can't tell forward from back because he does not know if there is a place he is supposed to go.

"I couldn't stand thinking about it. So I escaped to the streets, stole things, ran numbers for the wise boys. I fought in the ring, which made me keep my eye on what was in front and forget what was behind. And it felt good to hit somebody in the head. Even if I got hit in my own head it was better than at home.

"When that no longer worked I ran away to America. Where

149

else does a Jew run when life becomes impossible? I rode the rails all the way to the other side of the country. I discovered America. Huge brown rivers, roaring. Flat plains as wide and empty as the steppes. Mountains like you wouldn't believe. And the people? White, colored, English, Spanish, Jews, Gentiles, rich, poor, beautiful, smart, mean, stupid, open-handed, nasty, good-natured. A country to live a life in. My country now. Not just the Lower East Side of it. All of it, all the way to the other side and all the way back.

"I was in Syracuse when the War broke out. To get you to enlist they sold America the way you sell cheap suits. Advertising posters, men in sandwich signs, parades, flags, speeches, naked girls draped in flags on horse-drawn floats. All wasted on me. America was the least of my worries. All I wanted was to never go back to that crazy-house. Let the Army send me to France, four thousand miles away. Let them give me a gun and leave me to use it. If hitting and getting hit in the ring takes your mind off your troubles, think what killing and trying not to get killed will do! Also I remembered Jacob Shuster, leaning against the barricade and whistling while he cleaned his rifle. In this world a Jew must know how to fight, never mind what country he lives in.

"So I enlisted in the Regulars, the 38th Infantry. What we did in France . . . never mind. The important thing is this: when it was over I was ready to go back and face my brother Yossi. Because on account of the war I understood how it was with him.

"Things happened over there that were unbearable—to see, to feel, to remember. Murders with the gun, with the hand. How a person—a comrade, or even an enemy—how that person's body can be torn and made to suffer. When you do such things, and see them, and the pain of knowing them is beyond what you can stand, then you become Another, who stands apart from the person you were—become a man of wood, a *golem*, who walks and moves and kills but is responsible for nothing, who cannot feel the touch that wakes a man to pain.

"That's how I got through the war. And that must have been how Yossi got through being lost.

"Except that neither of us was truly made of wood. Inside us the person we used to be was still alive. So sometimes through the blank, through the wood, a memory would push itself out. He'd remember being lost, not knowing where he should go to find us, or if we were anywhere to be found, unable to tell the difference between forward and back. That's when Yossi would cry: 'He's falling through the air!'

"Not a dybbuk speaking," said Max. "A memory."

*A man turned inside-out. The trees full of dead people.*

"From the war I also had that kind of remembering. But these things had come to me as a man. When the memories come I can bear them. But Yossi suffered such things when he was a baby. The memories dragged him back to *lost* and he didn't have strength to escape. But maybe now with my understanding I could find a way to help him."

6

In the seven years Max was away Yossi had grown up. He was twenty. His response to Max's return was a brief twitch of the mouth, a smile cut off. After that he acted as if Max had never been away. He still had his spells of yelling crazy words, and of sitting still like a lump of wood for hours. But often he would sit calmly with his family, even talk a little back and forth—though he was always vigilant, as if words were enemies.

Max's parents were first shocked at his return, then bitter for his long desertion. They had lost the shop. Father, mother and son now earned their bread doing piecework in the apartment, three sewing machines chattering all day six days a week. "My father now looked like a Polish Hasid, beard to his waist, sidelocks, mumbling prayers of atonement. My mother's piety was fired by anger and grief, her prayers were like muttered curses. Sabbaths they went from one synagogue to another, seeking a rabbi with power to intercede with God on Yossi's behalf."

But what was the use of appealing to the kind of God who lets a child's life hang on whether he goes right or left? If something was to be done for Yossi, Max would have to do it.

He took note of his brother's strengths as well as his weakness. He saw the patience with which Yossi sat all day in that tiny apartment, stitching stitching stitching at his machine, intently watching the seams, his movements infinitely repetitive and meticulous. When he wasn't stitching he would draw designs on paper, fine networks of lines and curves—sit there drawing for hours, saying nothing, no sooner finishing one paper than he'd start another. Max asked him what they were. "Maps," he said, "they show the connections. How you go from here to anywhere." Maybe that kind of painstaking work absorbed Yossi's mind, the way fighting had kept Max from thinking about troubles that were too big for him to handle.

In 1922 Max was organizing for the Party, at a big factory that had its own design department. He showed the boss some of Yossi's work, and the boss said bring him around, they'd give him a try drafting patterns. For a few weeks Yossi was okay, copying patterns assigned by the master designer. Then the shit hit the fan. He refused to draw anything but his "maps," precisely calculated traceries spreading over the pages like the most complicated spider webs, each one wilder than the next. "My comrades there tried to talk him around, 'You got a good job, Yossi, *bend* a little.' Like talking to runaway train. He goes storming into the boss's office yammering a mile a minute, explaining his maps, explaining how they connected everything, how if you lose yourself in these maps you will never be lost."

"The boss calls security. They take Yossi by the elbows and put him out in the street.

"He disappeared.

"Finally I get a call from the 15th Precinct. He's been chalking crazy pictures on the sidewalks. When a cop tells him to move along Yossi springs on him, swinging his fists and screaming. I go to him in the jail—he hasn't cut his beard or hair for weeks, all matted and filthy and full of lice. I bail him out, we get him home. Two days quiet in his bed. Then my mother, from her own craziness, calls in a rabbi to scare the dybbuk out of him—and Yossi starts screaming at the rabbi and won't stop, screaming such terrible things that the holy man turns and runs for his life.

"So then it's Bellevue. He's in for a few weeks, they dope him up and talk to him, then let him out. If he's home three days he tears the place apart and runs for it—loses himself in the streets. The cops pick him up when they catch him haranguing people in front of churches, firing words like a machine-gun—vile, disgusting stuff about murders and shit and pigs. Then into Bellevue and out again. Like that, from 1922 to 1927.

"My dad develops a cough that puts him also into Bellevue, in the TB ward. He doesn't waste the opportunity: stops eating even when they bring him kosher food. Two weeks after we bury him my mother gets into her bed and turns her face to the wall.

"Yossi goes to live with Zeydeh in the basement of the house in Brooklyn. We try to make him part of the family. That picture you saw is from taking him on a picnic to Prospect Park in 1930. He's there, but he's not there. The hair sprouting out of his brain like his craziness. A week later he's gone again.

"This time he gets good and lost. Even the cops can't find him. I search all over the Lower East Side, from the river to the Bowery and back. Questioning the pushcart peddlers, did a crazy man try to swipe their stuff? Poking through the trash in the alleys, shining a flashlight around the basements. And then—I can't explain it—I get a picture in my head of the garbage dump in Lvov where I found him that time, impossible. So I go down to the dump they had then at the foot of Stanton Street, by the East River.

"And there he is, picking rotten potatoes and orange peels out of the dreck. When I call his name he looks at me and smiles. And gives me that wink—like it's a joke only the two of us understand.

"And I do. I understand. Because to him his life still turns on that small point, left or right, this garbage dump or that one. So he *goes back* to that place, and then maybe if someone comes and saves him then it was never just chance he got back to us, it was *supposed* to happen, it's the *rule*. Only he can't hold on to believing it. In the blink of an eye he goes lost again."

Like the Little Man who was *there* and *not-there*. In the end, everyone wished he would go away.

# 7

The Elders met in the living room of Zeydeh's house: Zeydeh, Abe and Mel, and Max. My father was not summoned—at sixteen he seemed to belong to his nephew Sherman's generation, rather than that of the Uncles. The exclusion of Aunt Rochelle had less excuse—the patriarchs were afraid of womanly appeals to their sympathies.

Because their verdict was a foregone conclusion: Yossi must be put away, for his own safety and the family's peace.

So what was there to discuss? The reason *why* Yossi was as he was.

Although they kept reminding themselves that the reason didn't matter—whatever it was, Yossi had to be put away—they could not rest easy with that verdict. There was a mystery in Yossi's fate too troubling to the conscience, too somehow dangerous, for them to leave it unresolved. Max shook his head, remembering. "He brought out all our own craziness. The only thing missing, thank God, was that with my mother and father gone we didn't have to consider miracles and dybbuks. But everything else was on the table."

Zeydeh sat hunched over, his eyes mournful. How could it be that after straining every nerve, devoting years of thought and perseverance and unstinting charity to bring his brother's family to safety—that in the end he must let his brother's youngest child fall into darkness? "But Yossi was happy living in my basement. In Russia you often saw such people walking in the street. Their families took care of them. Or the synagogue—or if it was goyim, the church."

"Papa," said Abe, and patted his father's hand to comfort him.

Mel snorted: "The village idiot. In Russia they have such an office. Not in Brooklyn."

Max couldn't let that pass. "He's not an idiot. He wasn't born crazy. He was a bright sweet little boy until he got lost. . . ." He tried to explain. It was important that they see Yossi for what he was, "so that even if we put him away, we don't lose sight of him, he doesn't vanish as if he'd never been."

But they didn't want to hear how it must have been for Yossi lost. Or about the terrible things he must have seen, and couldn't stop remembering. Abe waved his hand as if throwing the thought away. "But after all they *found* him. They *found* him. People suffer all kinds of things, they get over it. Life goes on."

Mel rolled his eyes. "No one in that family ever got over anything. They hugged their *tsores* like their dearest possession."

Max went red in the face. "You include me in this picture?"

Mel lifted a lip. "What should I say? Once upon a time you ran for the hills so as not to be part of it. But now you cling to this *farfalener geist*."

This lost ghost.

Zeydeh buried his face in his hands.

Abe rose to his father's brother's defense. "We can't blame Uncle Isaac and Aunt Sarah. They had no knowledge. You heard the doctors. There can be a sickness inside a person's brain—it waits, it doesn't show. It doesn't matter the life he leads, it's inside him. Then the man grows up and suddenly it springs out. He lets himself go." Abe shuddered. "He don't bathe or shave or cut his hair."

"And God forbid he ever comes by the store!" said Mel.

"*A shandeh for de goyim*," said Zeydeh, a shame on us all in the eyes of the Americans.

Max threw up his hands. "Thirty-five years in America and you're still walking tiptoe? Who cares what the goyim here think!

# Richard Slotkin

What can they do to you? You're Jews from Russia, you already know the worst that can happen. So go be American whatever way you like, and let the goyim bang their heads against a wall figuring out how to deal with it."

Mel glared at him. "You never understood what it means to be respectable!"

Abe asked for peace, a pressing-down motion with both hands as if extra strength was required to still the rancor. "Please! Let's speak calmly. This is not about us, it's about what's good for Yossi."

Mel turned their self-doubting and heartsick debate into a verdict: "What difference does it make whether it's craziness or memories that make him the way he is? Suppose it *is* memories. Let me tell you—in America, people don't have such memories. You have to get over those memories the way you get over a cholera or a typhus. If you don't, you're better off dead."

What was the use of arguing? Their choices were to let Yossi wander and rave himself to death on the streets, or put him where he could not harm himself or anyone else, and where with luck the doctors might find a way to mitigate his misery.

So Max consented, and they had Yossi committed to the Rockland State Hospital.

For everyone but Max, Mel's verdict was final. Once they put Yossi away they *put him away*. None of them ever went to visit him. He was alive, but never any more a part of their lives—like the son Mel sat *shiva* for, because he wouldn't become a certified public accountant.

"Yet to me he was still my brother Yossi. So every month I go up there, and sit with him, and look in his eyes. And next time we will go see him together."

## 8

The sprawling grounds of the Rockland State Hospital had been carved out of the woods just west of the newly opened Palisades Interstate Parkway. The administration building featured a central tower with flanking wings, and large arched windows with red-painted frames. But the blocks of buildings that lined up behind were uniformly dull in color and design, with grim rows of square windows on the upper floors.

On the ground floor of one of these buildings there was a large bright room where the patients could meet their visitors. The windows here were wide and tall, with rounded arches at the top, divided into small panes by an elegant network of steel bands. Only when you looked closely did you see that these bands were in effect bars, and that the glass was reinforced with chicken-wire between the double panes. The walls were decorated with paintings of scenes from New York State history—Robert Fulton's steamboat, the Erie Canal, the Statue of Liberty. The style was "primitive," as if childish taste was a feature of mental illness.

Max and I sat in a pair of chairs by one of the windows, and an empty chair awaited Yossi. I caught myself unconsciously wringing my hands—I was very nervous, not to say scared. Yossi was about to materialize. I guess I was expecting a figure worthy of the disgust Abe, Mel and Sherman had expressed, or of the terror that had driven Uncle Isaac and Aunt Sarah to throw themselves at the feet of the rabbis.

A door at the end of the room opened and two men entered: a patient dressed in a loose-fitting blue smock and pajama-pants, with worn leather bedroom slippers on his bare feet, followed by a Black attendant in a white jacket. The patient walked with an uneven shuffling slide, one shoulder higher than the other, the left leg dragging a little. When he came closer I could see fine small tremors run through his arms and hands.

Yossi. He was small, about five-five. His hair was gray, buzz-cut. Was that just the rigorous hospital style, or to make easier the affixing of electrodes for his shock therapy? His face shared Max's angular bone structure, but where Max's skin stretched tight as leather over jutting chin and bent nose and high cheekbones, Yossi's inmate-pale skin was soft and sagging. He looked ten years older than Max—was in fact six years younger. His cheeks were covered with a fine silver-gray stubble, which suggested that patients were only shaved every two or three days. If *beard* correlates with *insanity*, Yossi's condition was controlled but capable of sprouting.

The attendant stopped him when he reached the empty chair. "Say hello to your brother, Mister Joseph." Yossi's eyes were pale pale blue and flicked incessantly leftrightleftright, making no contact. A tap on the shoulder, and Yossi took his seat. The attendant promised to be back in a little while to give Yossi his medication.

Max waited a little, patiently, and after a time Yossi's flickering eyes would pause for a moment—hold briefly on Max's face then flit away again. Finally Max, choosing the moment to break his rhythm, smiled at Yossi. Not the clown-smile you spread for a simpleton or someone else's new baby, but the smile that springs when you meet after many weeks a good friend or a brother. "Yossele," he said softly.

"Max," said Yossi. "How come you're still here?" His voice was scratchy and a little flat, like an old phonograph record.

"No Yossele," he answered, "this is yet another time. I went away, then I came back to see how you're doing."

"You already asked me that," said Yossi, closing the subject.

"No Yossi, I didn't ask you yet. Like I said—this is a different time. Don't you remember? Last time I was here it was winter. Snow outside the window. Now it's spring—leaves on the trees."

Yossi raised an admonitory finger: "Don't talk about trees." *Dead men in the trees.*

"This is a new day," said Max, and pointed to me. "See? I brought your cousin Michael to visit you. I never did that before."

A tic in Yossi's cheek made him wink uncontrollably. His eyes flicked at me and away. "He's not lost, Max'l. If you can see him he's not lost."

"Of course he's not lost," said Max. "He was never lost. But why don't you tell Cousin Michael how they treat you here. He was worried about you." Max gently waved his open palm from me toward Yossi, inviting me to speak.

I nearly swallowed my tongue. There were a million questions I couldn't ask. What popped out was, "How's the food here?" which is what you ask a friend you're visiting in his dorm room.

The tic stopped. Yossi looked straight at me and raised an eyebrow. "It's crap. What do you expect? They cook it in a machine." It was one of those moments when Yossi became real to himself, *we know what really happened.*

Max laughed, and reached out to slap Yossi's knee. "I'll talk to the kitchen and get them to make you *kashe varnishkas*. Any other complaints?"

Yossi blinked, and you could see him fading out of his eyes. "They show bad movies here. Scary movies."

"What movies?"

"People turned inside out. Then the pigs come for them. You go flying away from everyone there is, and can't stop yourself."

Max looked grim. "But it's only movies, right Yossele? If I get them to stop showing the movies. . . ?"

Yossi shook his head. "They'll never stop." He looked at Max again with living eyes. "But it's only movies, Max."

On the way out we asked about the movies: the last one they'd shown was "The Prince and the Showgirl," with Laurence Olivier and Marilyn Monroe.

## 9

So that's the story of Cousin Yossi, our hidden shame, the little man who wasn't there. Neither his parents, nor his uncles, aunts and cousins, could bear to be with him or finally even to acknowledge his existence.

But to Uncle Max Yossi was neither miracle nor dybbuk, not the Angel of Death, nor even merely *a shandeh for de goyim*. Yossi was his brother, who had been horribly lost and strangely found, whose mind was so possessed by the memory of being lost that he could never be brought home. Max went right and lived, Yossi went left and was destroyed. It could have been the other way round— but it wasn't. History happens as it happens, not otherwise. God has nothing to do with it and neither has dialectical materialism. Take it from there. Take it personally.

So once a month for the rest of Yossi's life Max would come and sit with him, and look into his eyes—which were sometimes cold and dead as stone, and sometimes brilliant with horror, and sometimes which was hardest of all to bear would flash with recognition: *I know who you are. I know who I am. I understand what has become of me.*

# Greenhorn Nation: A History in Jokes

America is a nation of immigrants—thoroughly, from start to finish. No kind of human is native to the Americas. Our species evolved elsewhere. Those we call Native Americans are really just the First Nations, earliest on the ground, but they came from someplace else: from Asia via the Bering Strait land bridge or into the Fourth World through a hole in Mother Earth—as you prefer. The white-skin Colonials who created the United States of America like to think of themselves as "the real Americans." But in the eye of history they're just the Old White Settlers, the Second Nations in order of arrival, who dispossessed and incarcerated the First Nations. Black people arrived shortly after the Colonials. But they were not free emigrants—had been kidnapped in Africa and enslaved over here—so they were neither settlers nor immigrants. Call them the Third Nations, and imagine nations enslaved.

But when people use the phrase "nation of immigrants," they're usually referring to those of us who started arriving in the 1800s—after the Old White Settlers established their government, and began writing those ever more elaborate rules that govern the naturalization of newcomers: the Irish famine-folk and the German '48ers, the proletarians and peasants who stormed the seaports after the Civil War, the huddled masses yearning, the wretched refuse who streamed through Angel Island, Castle Garden and Ellis Island.

The difference between the Natives, the Old White Settlers, and the rest of us (*i.e.*, Blacks and immigrants) is that for the first

# Richard Slotkin

two nature itself, and not Ole Massa or the INS, worked on their minds and bodies and family ties, transforming Asians and Europeans into Americans. Later immigrants have to settle for "naturalization": a beautiful legal fiction, through which they gain the right to be treated *as if* they were native to the country.

Those of us born here of naturalized ancestors are heirs to that *as-if*-ness, our dual identities bridged by the Hyphen: Jewish-American, Italian-American, Asian-American, and so on till morning. When Black people, after two hundred and fifty years of slavery and a century of Jim Crow, finally attained something like civil equality, they became African-Americans—the award of the Hyphen signifying a change so extraordinary it was as if they had just (and finally) *arrived*. Welcome to America. Now get lost.

There is a modern school of thought which says, that over the decades since Ellis Island the Jews have "become White folks." No disrespect to the authors of these studies, but—I *know* White People. You don't *become* one of them if you start out as something else. Never mind that "White" is the only box you can check on your Census form. *As-if* is not the same as *born*.

Therefore the Hyphen is also a wedge that opens the way to ridicule. It marks us as pretenders to a freedom to which we lack the birthright. The freedom of African-Americans especially drives the Old White Settlers into paroxysms of hatred. Black people were *slaves*! That such despicable beings could *also* be free made the Settlers' own "freedom" look ridiculous. They would avenge that insult in blood, but also in kind. Hence the origin of the "Negro joke," in which even the most witless wheeze gets a laugh if the punch line is delivered in black-face dialect. Immigrants got a treatment similar in kind if not degree: jokes about Yids, Goombahs, Polacks, Chinamen, and the rest, whose ridiculous accents are a never-failing source of hilarity, a mockery of someone's pretensions to dignity.

But the jokes we others tell on ourselves play on the Hyphen like Miles on his horn, like Jascha on his Stradivarius.

162

# Greenhorns

The primal ethnic joke was probably made at the Bering Strait, when the first group of Stone Age hunters to cross looked back and saw the second group arriving. And it was still being told twenty thousand years later: Two Indians are crouched in the brush watching the Pilgrim greenhorns land at Plymouth Rock. Squanto turns to Massassoit and says, "There goes the neighborhood."

The irony and the humanity here is that, as each new set of greenhorns becomes naturalized, they assume the privilege of telling that same joke against any who arrive after them. The Yankee kids told it when the Irish got off the boat, and the Irish kids heard their parents tell it when the Jews and Italians moved in. The Jews and Italians repeated it when "that certain element" (i.e. Black people) tried to buy homes in their neighborhood, and I'm sure American-born Black people told it when the Dominicans and Puerto Ricans and Koreans showed up. They should change the national motto from "E pluribus unum" to "Finders Keepers."

In the process of naturalization, the immigrant and her descendants pass through several stages. The first generation are Greenhorns, an odd amphibian race living half in air and half in water, half on this side of the ocean and half on the other, at home in neither. They spend their lives scrabbling for a place in the nation, trying to figure it out and never quite getting it.

Later, when they're legally citizens, when they and their American-born children begin to move out of the ghetto and into the nation, they become "the You People"—as in, "Why don't *You People* stay with your own kind." Or "Don't *You People* know where you're not welcome?" The parents get one version of it, kids get another, as when the Irish toughs from Little Flower parish told me, "*You* people got no business this side of Forty-fifth Street." This after they took me down by running a stick into the spokes of my bike, and slashed my tires as punch line to the joke.

After the Greenhorn and the You People Stages comes the Feigenbaum Stage, which is named for the hero of a famous joke.

163

# Richard Slotkin

This is how I first heard it:

When I was a kid in the late 40s and early 50s, we lived in East Flatbush. Our neighborhood was mainly two-story attached houses made of brick and stucco on a street lined with big maple trees. My family, and the families of my father's two brothers, lived within three blocks of each other.

The largest of the houses belonged to Uncle Mike, and we would always go there for the first Passover Seder ("Once we were slaves unto Pharaoh in the Land of Egypt. . . ."). In fact, whenever there was a major event—a bar mitzvah, an engagement, a graduation—it had to be celebrated at Uncle Mike's in addition to whatever other party was arranged. Uncle Mike was, in his own words, "Chairman of the Board" in all family matters. It was a mantle he assumed as the eldest brother—but also the wealthiest, a CPA with an impressive clientele, while my father (the youngest brother) was a school teacher and Uncle Sam ran an auto repair shop.

Uncle Mike's house had the biggest backyard, with a patch of grass and a pear tree. So on sunny days in spring and summer we'd all gather there for a picnic, my mother and aunts bringing pitchers of iced tea, and dishes of stuffed cabbage, roast chicken, cold cuts, string beans and potato salad to the feast. Afterwards the brothers would sit in lawn chairs under the pear tree and talk and argue and tell stories. I was allowed to sit in—to listen, not to kibitz. They spoke freely, but shifted into Yiddish if the material was unsuitable to my young years.

Under the pear tree they also called each other by different names. Uncle Mike was "Meyer," Uncle Sam was "Shmuel," and my dad (who was usually called Hy) was "Chayim." At the time I thought these were Yiddish nicknames, used only in the intimacy of the family. When I was older—in fact, just before my bar mitzvah—my father told me these were in fact their birth-certificate names, given by their immigrant parents. Mike, Sam and Hy were their American aliases.

Mike was the tallest of the three, with a head of well-barbered

# Greenhorns

steel-gray hair. You almost never saw him wearing anything less formal than a suit. For picnics he doffed the jacket and tie, but still wore the starched white shirt, the pleated suit pants, the well-buffed shoes. He was always on his dignity, perhaps because he had a secret shame. Mike was the only brother born "on the Other Side"—a fact which was never to be mentioned in his presence.

Uncle Sam was a different type altogether—a Jewish Falstaff with a cigar in his mouth and a feaster's belly. He had left high school after one year to become a mechanic, and did well enough to own a fairly big garage near the terminal market, where the trucks came to pick up the goods unloaded from the freight cars. His jokes were robust, off-color, worth the belly laugh he gave them.

My father was the youngest and best educated. He had gone to college thanks to the GI Bill, but he wore his schooling lightly. He had a head of wild black Trotsky hair, a big nose with a rakish tilt to the side, and smiles came easily to him. He had a sharp eye, but a gentle nature. His jokes were really stories. They built a picture in your head, a situation that drew you in—then hit you with a kicker that turned the situation inside-out.

As a story-teller, Mike's specialty was the anecdote of human folly in the business world. These were worth a smile and a rueful roll of the eyes, but no real laughs. They lacked extravagance. His real role was as audience for his brothers' jokes—an awkward audience, because he didn't have their humor. He'd listen impatiently, clucking in disapproval at the antics of the fools in his brothers' stories, laugh just enough to be polite and to prove he understood everything even though he thought it was a waste of time and effort. I think that for Sam and my dad, half the fun was giving Brother Meyer the needle, and getting a rise out of him.

This particular session began as a conversation about Meyer's son Arthur, an accountant like his father, who had just signed on with a big firm in Miami and was moving South. How would he live without winter, how would he live without corned beef and pastrami? But these digs had already lost their force, because a

# Richard Slotkin

whole generation of New York Jews had either moved to Florida or were spending winters, and there was delicatessen enough for all.

Then the situation reminded my dad of this story:

It seems there was a family of Hasidic Jews in Brooklyn, the Feigenbaums. The grandfather and the fathers came over from Poland; the grandsons were born in America; they spoke Yiddish at home and English to the world. Over fifty years they developed a very successful chain of dry-goods stores, branches in all the Five Boroughs, in Boston and Philadelphia and the suburbs in between. The patriarch of the family believed it was time to expand beyond the northeast region. Cities were booming in the South and the Sunbelt! It was decided that the eldest son, Itzik Feigenbaum, should go to the City of Atlanta to make inquiries and see for himself whether or not that metropolis was suitable for a Feigenbaum's franchise.

So Itzik gets off the train and walks through downtown Atlanta for an appointment with a local banker. It's the height of the day, ferociously hot, and he's wearing full Hasidic regalia: the long black wool coat over black wool pants and black shoes, white shirt and black tie, on his head a wide-brimmed pot-crowned black velour hat. His milk-white face is framed by an explosion of bushy flame-red beard and by carrot-red sidelocks that hang like lengths of sausage and sway as he walks. As he passes heads turn, black heads, white heads. They throw at him everything from shy side-long inquisitive glances to full-out jaw-dropped pop-eyed gawks.

Itzik begins to be annoyed.

But he keeps his composure.

He gets to the bank. The receptionist practically leaps from her seat in surprise, turns three shades of purple, gasps out a greeting; then pulls herself together and leads him to the Vice President's door. *Knock knock.*

The door opens.

The Vice-President rises from behind his desk—gets a load of Itzik and he's so startled his head snaps back on his neck and the eyes bug out of his head.

166

# Greenhorns

That's the last straw for Itzik. "Vhawts de matteh," he says, "ain't you never seen a *Yenkee* before?"

Uncle Sam threw back his head and roared. Uncle Mike pursed his lips and shook his head. "A greenhorn!" he said, "With whiskers like a goat! A greenhorn fresh from the Kesselgarden."

These were Uncle Mike's terms of utter contempt. "The Kesselgarden" was Castle Garden—originally a fortress, then an antebellum entertainment palace where Jenny Lind sang arias, and Irishmen who need not apply patted juba in blackface; and after that it served as the processing center for immigrants arriving in New York by sea. It had become a Yiddish by-word for mass confusion and disorder, a Babel teeming with not-so-fresh immigrants fresh off the boat, smelling of steerage and poverty. A greenhorn newly emerged from that stew was, for Uncle Mike, a thing to be scorned. As it happens, the Kesselgarden later became the New York Aquarium—tanks of fish, each with its own kind, swimming round and round without a word to say for themselves. Which is also an American Dream.

But Feigenbaum! "It's a joke, Meyer," Sam cried. "You're allowed to laugh."

Uncle Mike was annoyed. "A greenhorn makes a fool of himself and the shame comes back on the rest of us."

That set the brothers laughing again, and I joined them. It tickled me that Uncle Mike, with all his stiff dignity, looked silly for not getting the joke. I also laughed at Feigenbaum's dopey self-confidence, walking around looking like that and having no idea what real Americans would think of him. It didn't occur to me at the time that my take on Feigenbaum was essentially the same as Uncle Mike's.

But it's one thing to laugh when you're outside the joke looking in; when you're inside it you laugh out the other side of your face.

That same summer our family took a driving tour down to Miami to visit Cousin Arthur and enjoy his ample new ranch house and its private swimming pool. I was just beginning to be an enthusiast for American history, so Dad mapped out a tour that began with a visit to the Gettysburg battlefield park, and to Washington, DC, before plunging into Dixie. At Gettysburg the Civil War came alive for me. My younger brother and I climbed all over the Federal artillery on Cemetery Ridge, stared down the sights across the valley to where life-size statues suggested Pickett's brigades just emerging from the woods to charge the high ground. For the first time I felt *placed* in American history, as if in some way my own life, or some essential part of my identity, had been at stake in a battle that happened decades before my ancestors landed here. William Faulkner once wrote that for every Southern boy (meaning *white* Southern boy) it was always possible to go back in imagination to Gettysburg, in the moments before Pickett's Charge, when it was still possible that the South and slavery might win the Civil War. The same would now be true for me—except that I would be with the Union guns on Cemetery Hill, waiting impatiently for the chance to blow the Confederacy to hell.

Our visit to DC, and the Lincoln Memorial, turned those visions into a vocation. Lincoln had always been an iconic figure for our family, as he was for most Jews—Lincoln freed the slaves and "Once *we* were slaves unto Pharaoh in the Land of Egypt." When I was very young I assumed he was Jewish, the namesake of my grandpa Abe on my mother's side. On my bedroom wall at home was a picture my dad had brought back from a Jewish War Veterans' meeting, and had framed for me: the Matthew Brady image of Lincoln's haggard prophetic face, and next to it "Dedicated to the proposition that all men are created equal." You have to remember that I was born during the War, and had my childhood in an atmosphere saturated with visions of America as the liberator of a world once enslaved to fascism and imperialism, and later as the defender of a Free World menaced by Red Communism. Now I gazed at shaggy, colossal Abraham in his temple, his stern intent gaze down the whole length of the Mall keeping watch on the Capitol, judging whether or not his successors were living up to the standard he set. I was going to do something worthy of Lincoln when I grew up.

Then we drove south, through the Shenandoah Valley of Virginia, and stopped at Luray Caverns. We toured the caves, and afterwards I had to pee. So while the family riffled through souvenir postcards at the reception desk, I skipped off and into the first bathroom I saw with the outline figure of a man on it.

As I came in a Black man stepped out of one of the stalls— jerked back in shock at the sight of me. His face went furious just like that, and he growled, "Boy you better get yourself out of here *now*!" He was mean-looking and mad, and I turned and bolted back out the door.

To run straight into the glare of the uniformed woman receptionist. She was red in the face, and shaking with anger. "You people! You people think you can come down here and just do anything you please!"

"What's the trouble?" my mother asked.

"Can't you people read a sign?" she snapped, and pointed toward the bathrooms. Above the door I'd entered was a sign that said MEN COLORED ONLY. The door next to it said, MEN WHITES ONLY.

My mother hustled my brother and me out through a mass of murmuring tourists while my father fought some kind of rear-guard action. I was shaking, with fear of course but mostly with humiliation. I had never done anything so outrageously bad that strange grown-ups would have felt justified in screaming at me—in front of hundreds of people!

We drove away from that place, miles down the road, then stopped at a roadside picnic table. I knew my mom and dad were thinking what to say to me, sitting side by side in the front seat, throwing looks back and forth, whispering a word now and then. I knew they would try to explain what I'd done wrong in a way that would soften the shame and the rebuke—and knowing they'd try that, I already believed it wouldn't work.

For some reason my dad was the one who would do the explaining. He sat down next to me on the picnic bench, and put his arm around me. "That woman yelled at you, because you broke the rules they have down here. I know you didn't do it on purpose. And even if you did—they're stupid rules, they're actually very bad rules. But they're the law down here, so we have to be careful about them." I told him that the Black man in the bathroom yelled at me too, and he got a funny look on his face. "He was probably more scared than anything—scared he'd get blamed . . ."

. . . and then he tried to explain to me about segregation and Jim Crow. When I say "explain," I don't mean justify. All he did was state the facts. In the South the law didn't let Black people go to the same schools as White people, sit in the same seats on trains and buses or in movie theaters, drink from the same fountains. And also that Black people mostly were not allowed to vote. And sometimes White people killed them for no reason.

But how could this be? We had just seen the Lincoln Memorial and Gettysburg, which were supposed to prove that all that nastiness had ended in 1865—that we had gained the power to save the world from Hitler because our hearts had been purified and our hands made clean. Then why would Americans . . . why would *grown-ups*, who in my experience were almost uniformly kind and reasonable, allow such a thing?

I suppose this is "the conversation" every American boy or girl must, at some point, have with their parents—not the one about sex, the one about race. And like the sex conversation, boys had to have it with their fathers, and girls with their mothers—or so it was back then. You can't raise children in America without having to have that conversation sooner or later. But it must happen very differently in our country's varied households, and come to different conclusions, and maybe in most of them it's a conversation without words. In our case, my dad didn't try to explain how this unreasonable and unjust condition had come to be—he just laid it out for me, and left it to me to figure out what to think, and what I must say, and what I must do about it. Now it occurs to me that this was a gift, like the picture of Lincoln he'd brought back from the JWV meeting.

The conversation finally wore itself out, we hit the road again, and I dozed a little, exhausted—then was jerked awake by fear and anger when it came back to me how that receptionist had humiliated me! *You people think you can come down here and. . . .*

But wait. When she said *You people*, did she mean me as a Yankee? Or me as a Jew?

And that was when I finally got the Feigenbaum joke—which also defines the Feigenbaum Stage of naturalization—which is: that even without the beard and the sidelocks, even with a mind crammed so full of America that you can't think of yourself as anything else, you're still strolling the streets with your Hyphen hanging out. Put anything you like in front of the Hyphen, Jewish- or Polish-, African- or Chinese-, Lebanese- or Japanese-, you will someday run into someone who has never seen your kind of Yankee before. And God bless you if, like Feigenbaum, you can walk away thinking it's the other guy who's made a fool of himself.

So what do you make of that? What do you make of yourself?

I would make myself a student of American history. Unlike William Faulkner, I was not born to my Gettysburg dream. I had to earn the right to imagine myself among the Union guns, or marching through Georgia to destroy slavery at the root—earn it by mastering all the history that culminated in those moments, and all the history that came in consequence; and earn as well the right to interpret America, to explain and to create its meanings.

In college I majored in American Studies, and went on to study for my PhD in that field. But in the university culture of the early 1960s that sense of calling, and the intensity with which I pursued it, marked me as alien. The pre-eminent scholar in my chosen area

# Richard Slotkin

of American history was Professor Carl Bridenbaugh, who (in an address he gave on his 1962 election to the presidency of the American Historical Association) had declared that the younger generation of "urban-bred" historians, of "lower-middle-class or foreign origins," lacked the intuitive sense of nationality that allowed them grasp the essence of American culture. "They find themselves, in a very real way, outsiders in our past, and their emotions frequently get in the way of their historical reconstructions."

In other words, they were greenhorns. And as such, no more welcome sit at the table with *American* American historians than that Black man had been welcome to pee in a Whites Only bathroom.

And yet, to give Professor Bridenbaugh his due, my "lower-middle-class or foreign origins" do give a peculiar emotional energy to my quest for knowledge. My American identity rides on the edge of a knife. If my father's father had had a little less gall, been a little less shrewd, been favored a little less by fortune, I would have no American history. My family and I would be nameless dead in a Gulag cemetery, would be smoke, ashes and soap, would be a snarled heap of bones smothered in a trench. The same holds for my wife and her family, and for the families of all our relatives, all our childhood friends.

As the heir of that heritage I find that being American is not an identity I can ever take for granted. It is something to be worried over and worked at. There are times when I feel as American as Abraham Lincoln or Tom Sawyer. And there are times when I'm a complete greenhorn, astonished by the discovery of some new American wonder or estranged by the eruption of one of our society's latent horrors, to which "real" Americans seem indifferent or inured. My own life *is* at stake in the travails of the Republic, and was even in the centuries before my ancestors landed here. If Americans did not learn from their history to reject African slavery, and the racial injustice that flowed from it, how could the nation be safe harbor for *my* people's exodus from bondage? The Trail of Tears showed that even natives born could be expelled if their

172

differences marked them as aliens in a White-man's republic. If Americans could not see that as injustice, what safety then for immigrant Yids and their children? If America is indeed a kind of Zion, still I am not at ease in it. I leave it to you whether that is a liability or an advantage for a historian.

But that brings me to the last stage of naturalization—the name of which I can't tell you yet, because it's the punch line of the joke.

This was one Uncle Sam told under the pear tree in Uncle Mike's yard, either that summer or another just like it. It was the kind of joke that was certain to get Mike's goat, coarse and earthy and resting on a premise so irrational it was an insult to Uncle Mike's double-entry book-keeping intelligence.

It seems that two old Jews named Shmulka and Avrom became best friends, living as they did in the Brooklyn Hebrew Home for the Aged. They were both well into their eighties, they'd known bad times on the Other Side and hard times on this one—so many shared experiences of loss, and striving, and loss again, it was as if they'd been brothers.

Their true lives were all behind them—wives and siblings gone, children scattered out into the American distance. Now what they had, and had in common, were the diseases, the chronic conditions, the complaints of cranky old men. Appetite? For what—the *dreck* they serve in this place? Physical comfort? Their kishkes had turned to wood, it took a whole morning on the crapper straining like a stevedore to crank out three little goat-beans. As for sex—if there had been in that place even one woman with some juice left in her, and vision dim enough to mistake these two broken grasshoppers for desirable males, they could have done nothing about it. Their lust was buried with their wives. What was left of their schlongs hung limp as a pair of wet noodles.

"Ach," said Uncle Mike, "that's disgusting!"

"My point exactly," Sam replied.

With all that they had lost, what did these two old farts have but each other? And yet it was certain that one day one of them would die, and leave the other bereft. So they made a pact. If there was indeed an Afterlife, a Heaven, whichever of them was the first to pass over would somehow contrive to contact the other—to comfort the survivor with the promise of reunion.

And it came to pass, as Moses says, that one day Shmulka failed to rise from his bed. The shock nearly killed Avrom, and he plunged down a long slide of despair as he realized his comrade was utterly lost to him. Shmulka's family, which before had hardly ever been seen at the Brooklyn Hebrew Home for the Aged, swept in in a mob, stole the body away for a funeral way out on Long Island, too far from the Home for its bus service to transport Avrom. None of the family thought to offer him a ride. So Avrom sat shiva for his friend all alone in his little apartment.

This Avrom was cursed with a health too good to let him die and too miserable to let him enjoy his life. Two years later he still lingers—constipated, sleepless, taking no pleasure in food or family or his fellow Jews. And then one night when he has *finally* dozed off . . . the phone rings!

Avrom picks up, angry as dog with fleas, "What!? Who the hell calls you this time of night!?"

"Avrom!" says the voice, "Avrom it's me!"

"My God," he says, "Shmulka! Shmulkele! Can this be real? Can it be you?"

"It's me, Avrom," says Shmulka. "I promised I'd call you, and I kept my word. And how are you, my dearest friend?"

"How should I be?" says Avrom. "The same as all the days we were together. But what about you? What is it like where you are?"

"Ah," says Shmulka, "you wouldn't believe it! All day I roam through fields of grass and wild-flowers every color. I eat what I please, and it pleases me to eat—whenever I want, and all that my belly can hold. And when I shit—my God, it's like dumping great loads of potatoes down a chute, rolling and thundering out!"

"How wonderful!" Avrom moans, "I can hardly imagine it!"

# Greenhorns

"And Avrom—I have a new family, children and *grand*children—they follow me wherever I go, I'm never alone. And better yet...." His voice dropped to a whisper: "The sex! Avrom, the sex! I've got a cock the size of a baseball bat, and dozens of females all around me, ready and willing!"

"My God," cries Avrom, "so that's what Heaven is like?"

"What Heaven?" says Shmulka—"I'm a buffalo in Wyoming!"

My dad laughed his head off, but Meyer made a face like he was in pain. "It's just vulgarity—and it makes no sense, 'a buffalo in Wyoming.' How is that an Afterlife?" Dad tried to explain about reincarnation, but that was for Hindus, so Meyer still couldn't see the sense of it. "And anyway—how does a *buffalo* make a phone call?"

Point taken.

But if you think of "A Buffalo in Wyoming" as what follows the Feigenbaum Stage, it makes perfect sense. What form of naturalization could make a greenhorn more thoroughly American than transformation into a buffalo—a species that, unlike humankind, is truly native to the American continent, evolved here from some prototype rodent who scurried among the fanged toes of tyrannosaurs. The Buffalo-in-Wyoming Stage! To be finally, undeniably, unmistakably American, and enjoy the good American life—to have wide-ranging freedom in a world that satisfies all needs—for the greenhorn Jew and his heirs, that's Heaven.

Of course, the symbol of that dream is a creature that was hunted with genocidal ferocity and nearly exterminated by the Old Settlers, in aid of their program for breaking the First Nations and locking them in open-air ghettos.

So even in our American dreams the Hyphen persists and binds us to the other side.

# Acknowledgements

The stories in *Greenhorns* are based on the real experiences of family members who came to the US from Russia or Poland between 1900 and 1921. I am grateful to Maurice and Gussie Shupack, Roselyn and Herman Slotkin, Elke and Sam Granit, George and Fannie Seplowitz, and Norma Brown for sharing their stories with me. Thanks also to my agent, Henry Thayer, for his hard work and good advice; and to Iris, Joel and Caroline for their encouragement on this project.

"The Other Side" was published in *Jewishfiction.net*, Number 19, Fall 2017, http://www.jewishfiction.net/index.php/publisher/articleview/frmArticleID/531

The quotations from Professor Bridenbaugh's AHA Presidential Address are in Carl Bridenbaugh, "The Great Mutation," *American Historical Review* 68:2 (January 1963), 315-31.

# Reader's Guide to GREENHORNS

1. The main characters in these stories have very different ideas about America—different ideas about what they will find there, different ideas about the kind of country America is.

   Discuss some of these differences.

2. In "The Gambler" Aaron bets "everything he had in life to win his family safe to America, and in winning he lost." He throws up his hands. "Let the sages unravel it."

   But how would you judge the success or failure of his gamble?

   At any point, could he have done better?

3. How does Aaron's absence affect his marriage to Sarah?

4. In "The Other Side" we see the new life Bella has made for herself, and the horror from which she escaped, but aren't told much about her early life in America.

   What elements in her character and her past enabled her to transform herself?

5. In "Honor" the boy narrator is torn between two ideas of honor—his father's version, and an "American" version, learned in the schoolyard.

   What is the practical difference?

   The moral difference?

6. How does the narrator's experience with the Cossack affect his actions and his sense of honor?

# Richard Slotkin

7. In "Milkman" Zeydeh describes one way of making "an American."

   Compare his method with the experiences of other immigrants like Aaron, or the boy narrator of "Honor."

8. How does the father's experience of being an immigrant affect the narrator of "Children, Drunks, and the United States of America"?

   How do the narrator's experiences in Mexico, and his dealings with Kid Kelleher and Yarbrough, affect his understanding of what it means to be American?

9. Why does the family in "Uncle Max and Cousin Yossi" deny Yossi's existence?

   Why is Max's attitude different?

10. In "Greenhorn Nation," why does the writer propose changing the national motto from *E pluribus unum* to *Finders Keepers*?

11. America is often described as "a Nation of immigrants."

    To what extent is the experience of these Jewish immigrants representative of immigrant experience in general?

12. The story "Greenhorn Nation" is subtitled "A History in Jokes."

    How should we understand the "punch line," the last line in the story?

13. In all of these stories, immigrants and their children have a problematic relation to those they think of as "real Americans" —but they express different ideas about who "real Americans" are, and how they relate to strangers.

# Greenhorns

Discuss the differences—and the consistencies—in the portrayal of "real Americans."

14. If you had to go and live in another country, what would you be most worried about?

# Author

Courtesy of Bill Burkhardt

Richard Slotkin has been recognized as one of the leading scholars of American cultural history, and as a historical novelist. His novel *Abe* (2000) won the Michael Shaara Prize for Civil War Fiction and the Salon Book Award; and *The Crater* was the first novel to be made a selection of the History Book Club. Both novels were *Times* "Notable Books of the Year." His non-fiction includes: *Regeneration Through Violence* (1973), which won the Albert Beveridge Prize of the American Historical Association and was a National Book Award Finalist; *The Fatal Environment* (1985), which won the Little Big Horn Associates Literary Award; and *Gunfighter Nation* (1992), a National Book Award Finalist. He taught for more than forty years at Wesleyan University, and in 1995 received the American Studies Association's Mary Turpie Award for his work as teacher and program builder. He retired in 2008 as Olin Professor of American Studies (Emeritus).

CPSIA information can be obtained
at www.ICGtesting.com
Printed in the USA
BVHW03s0506250818
525137BV00002B/6/P

9 781935 248996